Unpuzzling The Past

Mary L. Chase and Mary Davis

Published by Mary Davis, 2024.

Mary Davis, *Unpuzzling the Past*

Acknowledgements:

Special thanks to Sarah Yergin, Kathleen E. Kovach, Suzanne Norquist, and Jessica Robbins. You guys are awesome!

Published by Mary Davis

Copyright © 2024 by Mary Davis

All rights reserved. No part of this book may be used or reproduced in any manner without written permission, except in the case of brief quotations embodied in critical articles and reviews.

Copy edited by: Jessica Robbins

Cover design by Jessica Robbins

Visit http://marydavisbooks.com

Dedication

Since Mary Linn Chase isn't here to dedicate this book to anyone, I, Mary Davis, will speak on her behalf. "For my sister Sarah. Thanks for finding a way to get my book published. Love, Mary Linn."

I, Mary Davis, would also like to dedicate this book to all our relatives and hope they enjoy it. A special thanks to my mom and sisters for encouraging me along the way. And huge thanks to Kathy and Suzanne, my critique partners, for keeping the details straight.

About This Book

Dear Reader,

I have been given a gift—a gift of an unedited novel written by a family member (my first cousin once removed) who passed away many years ago. It had many issues we all made early in our writing endeavors. However, the plot was well thought out and kept me reading to find out what happened. The technical things could be fixed. Many people say they want to write a book and never do. Others start but never see it to the end. However, *finishing* a book is *huge* and an incredible accomplishment. Add a good plot on top of that, and I am impressed by my cousin's work.

The author's sister, Sarah, gifted it to me, saying it needed a lot of editing and I could do whatever I wanted with it—even throw it away. When I received it in the fall of 2020, I needed to finish my contracted novels first. In February of 2022, I was finally in a position to read it. Though it did need extensive editing, it was definitely worth the effort.

Then I dove in and started cleaning up a few things. When I was about a third of the way or so through it, I realized the timeline had major issues. This story takes place around Christmas, and it spanned the two-week period between Christmas and New Year's. The problem being there is only one week between those two holidays. We have all been there in our writing. We either have too many days in a week or have events take place on a Tuesday and the next day is Sunday. A few days got lost in there.

So, I stopped, read through the entire manuscript again, and filled out a notecard for each chapter with the events that happened in it. I needed to squish two weeks into one. I started reorganizing the events so I could figure out what day of the week would be best to have Christmas fall on. Which then let me know what possible year this story could take place in and use part of the week before Christmas. This gave me nearly the two weeks needed for the story. Some of the events are more condensed than real life to include all the major plot points, but this is fiction, after all. Unfortunately, I didn't have the advantage of being able to talk these things over with the author. So, I jumped into the major task of reordering all the scenes and started back at the beginning with editing.

It was a lot of work to remove all the little incidental references from where they no longer belonged and move them to where they did belong. But it was worth it.

Since it had no title, it was up to me to give it a name. I had toyed with several and waffled a lot. So, I took a vote. I offered up my top two options to the author's sister and decided whichever one she chose was the title that was meant to be.

I hope you enjoy *Unpuzzling the Past*.

Blessings,

Mary Davis

=0)

Chapter One

December 21, 1998

The second Christmas without Mom wasn't any less lonely than the first. Perhaps that was the reason Margaret Ross paced from the living room to the kitchen, waiting for her best friend. That and a huge family mystery that had swept over her like a tsunami yesterday. At this rate, she would wear a hole right through her hardwood floors. What on earth was taking Mindy so long? One would think that at nearly age thirty Mar would have learned more patience.

She juggled the pieces of recently acquired information in her mind. A baffling puzzle. Stopping at the front window, she peered out at the cloudy day. Just four days before Christmas, the weatherman predicted cold and cloudy but no snow for the holiday, which was fine by her. Seattleites weren't known for successfully traversing icy roads.

At long last, her friend pulled up in front of Mar's house. She stepped out of her Chevy Blazer in full rain regalia, even though it wasn't currently raining, and sauntered along the walkway as though this were any ordinary morning.

Finally.

Until college, she and Mindy had been inseparable pals since meeting in first grade.

When her best friend reached the porch, Mar flung open the door and grabbed her by the arm, almost jerking her into the entrance hall. "Get in here. I need to talk to you."

Mindy stumbled inside. Her mouth dropped open, rendering her mute, but she recovered quickly. "Wh-what's happened? You seem upset."

Taking a deep breath, Mar steadied her nerves. "You know I've been meaning to do something with Mom's things ever since she died last year before Christmas."

"Yes, what about it?" Mindy flipped back her hood, then her eyes widened. "Did you find a stash of cash or something? I know you're still trying to scrape up enough money to start your own advertising agency."

"No, no, it's nothing like that." The plethora of new information tumbled around chaotically in Mar's head. "But it's really important. Come on, let's get away from this drafty old hall. We can go into the kitchen, and I'll make some hot chocolate to warm you up while I try to explain. Although, I'm not sure if I quite believe it myself."

"Wait." Mindy held up her hands. "Let me take off my coat."

When she removed her yellow rain slicker, Mar hung it on the coat tree. After her friend stepped out of her blue rubber boots, Mar took her hand. "Come on."

Mindy planted her feet and grinned. "Ready."

"Aren't we a little old for this?"

"Never. We've always had carpeting in our house, your floors are fun."

Funny how life was. Mar had always envied Mindy for having wall-to-wall carpeting. So much warmer than cold, hard wood beneath her feet with a scattering of area rugs. She pulled Mindy along behind her as she hurried toward the kitchen.

"Wee!"

At the threshold, Mar released her friend as a giggle escaped her.

Mindy joined in. "I needed that. I've been so serious and focused on my studies, I haven't had time for anything else. Good to know I haven't forgotten how to laugh."

Mar opened the cupboard and pulled down two mugs. "Let's warm you up."

"I'm not cold. My blue wool slacks are toasty, and my cheery red and white ski sweater is cozy." Mindy raised a foot clad in a fuzzy, red toe-sock. "*And* I have on my reindeer socks."

"Well, we both know how powerful those are." Mar heaved a sigh.

"I haven't seen you this solemn since your mother fell ill and passed away." Mindy settled into a white kitchen chair with the comfortable blue and white gingham pads. "Now, what's this all about?"

Mar turned toward the stove and poured the beverage. She handed her best friend one of the bright stoneware mugs steaming with hot chocolate. "You won't believe it. Oh, Mindy, it just can't be true. I can't wrap my head around it."

Mindy twisted her face. "What on earth are you talking about? If you don't get to the point soon, I'm going to go home and leave you to stew in your own juice. Then who will you talk to?"

Mar slumped into the adjoining chair. "Don't even make a joke about it. You remember how I've left things in Mom's room pretty much as she had them. I never wanted to take the time or trouble to go through everything. It sort of allowed me to feel as though she was still around, just on a trip or something."

"I'm sorry for being impatient." Mindy patted her hand. "Go on."

"It was such a gloomy day, and I'm all done with my Christmas chores. I decided to dig around in Mom's closet and dresser drawers and pick out some things for the women's shelter. Sort of Mom's gift to them. I think she would like that." Mar gave assistance to the organization and individual women in need.

"*Annnd?*" Mindy stood and crossed to the teddy bear jar on the counter. "What about it? You've been meaning to do that for ages." She tucked a butter cookie between her lips and held out a second one.

Mar waved the offer away. She had eaten far too many of them while baking. "I found a lot more than I expected, and I don't know whether to believe any of it or not. Stay here. I have most of it gathered in one place. I'll show you, then you can see for yourself." Not waiting for a comment, she dashed off down the hall to Mom's old room.

In seconds, she returned and plopped a fat manila envelope onto the table, bumping the pot of red and white poinsettias.

Mindy clasped her hands around the container, keeping the plant upright.

"Thanks. Nice save." Mar dumped out the envelope's contents. A couple of old diaries thudded to the table's surface, along with a bunch of photos and some legal papers fastened together with huge rubber bands. "Journals, documents, and marriage certificates, even birth certificates." She picked up the yellowing documents. "It's like a giant jigsaw puzzle, but some of the pieces are missing and others don't seem to fit at all, not anywhere." She vaguely remembered her mom handling some of these things in the year leading up to her passing. Mom must have realized she didn't have much time, and this was her way of getting her affairs in order.

Mar sat down to the pile of papers, pushing their chocolates aside. "Look here." Picking up one of the diaries, she flipped it open and pointed. "It's kind of cramped writing, but I can tell Mom wrote it. There are letters from Dad mixed in with the pages that go back to before I was born. I always thought they were married long before I came along, but now it seems they weren't. Dad's draft orders got messed up, and he suddenly had to ship out to Vietnam before the wedding."

Setting aside the journal, Mar rifled through the legal papers. "Here's an unused marriage license with some of the information filled in that I found folded up with the certificate from the real wedding. They always celebrated on the first date even though the actual marriage took place more than two years after my birth." A lump of emotion made itself known in her chest.

She must have looked as dejected as she felt because Mindy took her hand. "Don't feel bad. Lots of people are born before their parents are legally married, and at least, you know they intended to get hitched. It was merely the circumstances which prevented them."

"Oh, that's not it." Regardless of when they got married, they were still her parents. Mar heaved a sigh. "There's a lot more here than you can even imagine." She waved her arm over the chaos strewn across the table. "While reading the diaries and letters, then checking the documents, I discovered I was one of two babies. A *twin*! I always wanted a sibling. But what happened to my brother or sister?"

Mindy's expression transformed from concern to wide-eyed shock. "Are you sure? How do you know?"

"Pretty sure." It was so unreal, Mar doubted herself over and over. Picking up another one of the books, she opened it. "Look at this." She pointed to a page filled with more of the small, cramped writing. "It seems as though Mom didn't know where to send her letters to Dad, so she copied her daily letters to him in her diary. This part explains she'd been to see old Dr. Thomas and found out they were expecting a child. He offered to deliver the baby at home to reduce costs, allowing them to pay when Dad returned and everything got straightened out. The pages tell how she misses him, but that she's getting along. She was always cheerful and tried to paint a bright picture. You know Mom, she invariably had a smile on her face."

Mindy held up her hand. "Wait a minute. Did women give birth at home in the sixties?"

"Not normally, but a few did. Mom was barely scraping by, so Dr. Thomas and his wife were trying to help her out. Since Mom and Dad weren't married, and Dad's military request form had gotten lost, they wouldn't send his pay to her."

"Typical bureaucracy. I wouldn't be surprised if they *lost* it on purpose because they weren't married."

Mar shook her head. "That's all beside the point and off track. It doesn't matter why she gave birth at home." She thumped her index finger on the diary. "There is an entry where Mom says the doc heard *two* heartbeats. *Two*."

Mindy's eyebrows lifted. "Twins?" She stared at Mar for a long time. "Like you, I'm having a hard time grasping all this." Finally, she choked out the words. "Then what happened? Did your twin die?"

"I haven't found proof either way." Mar's throat tightened with emotion as well at the prospect of that being the case. "There isn't a birth *or* death certificate for the other baby. I've never heard of a grave or even that there was a second child. Only me."

"What does your mom say in her diaries?"

"She says both babies cried after they were born. Dr. Thomas and his wife told her the second one died soon after the delivery. However, Mom didn't remember seeing the dead baby, but she was worn out from a long, hard labor. It's as though the other baby never existed. She wrote to Dad about the whole thing."

"This doesn't make sense. An infant can't simply disappear. Legally, there has to be some record of it. Both the birth *and* death."

Mar took a deep breath before continuing. "The doctor and his wife said they would take care of the little body so she wouldn't have any more worries or expenses. Though it seemed like a good idea when she was in such bad shape, later, she wondered. By then the old doctor had died, and now his practice has been sold. I went to the clinic first thing today when they opened to see if I could locate her records."

"Now we're getting somewhere." Mindy sat up straighter.

But it wasn't so. Mar shook her head. "No one seems to have any idea what has happened to Mom's old records. The new doctor was out, and his office nurse—a snippy redhead named Patty—acted as though I was crazy or something. She said I had no right to even ask about them, and they destroyed all the old records. The only ones they kept were for active patients."

Mindy squinted. "I don't think that's legal. I'm pretty sure they're required by law to keep them for a certain number of years. Just in case. At least, microfilmed for storage."

"I suspect they weren't destroyed. Mrs. Thomas is about ninety now but still alive." Mar had gotten more upset with every sentence, and now, she felt ready to collapse on the spot.

Her friend shook her head in what appeared to be confusion. "How do you know all that if you only found this stuff yesterday?"

Mar had been very busy since discovering the stash of information. "Well, I started yesterday after church and resumed pretty early this morning." Had it really been less than twenty-four hours since this whole mystery began? It felt more like a week. "I'll admit I haven't gone over the diaries and letters with a fine-tooth comb. When I figured out how to match the dates, I put two and two together." Once she'd gotten started, the momentum had propelled her forward like a runaway train.

Somewhere around three a.m. this morning, Mar had drifted off and slumped over the documents on the table. "I remembered reading old Mrs. Thomas had been moved to Orchard Park Nursing Home and decided to take a chance. I hurried over there and talked a staff member into allowing me to visit with her. The nurse felt bad for the old woman because she rarely had visitors. Anyway, I saw Mrs. Thomas, and she either doesn't know or isn't about to tell me anything. Then this morning, I went to the clinic she and her husband had run for years. I've told you about Nurse Snippy, so you know that didn't take long. Then I came home and waited for you."

"If that nurse disliked you without cause, then I dislike her *with* cause." Mindy retrieved her hot chocolate from the edge of the table and took a sip. "Tell me about your visit with Mrs. Thomas. I wish I had been there."

Mar wished that too, but she'd been too anxious to get answers to wait until her friend arrived. "At the nursing home, the staff assured me Mrs. Thomas was okay and told me where to find her. I hustled right back to her room and explained who I was. She seemed confused at first but eventually admitted she vaguely remembered Mom." Mar halted long enough to take a deep breath. "However, she couldn't—*or wouldn't*—acknowledge there'd been twins. I couldn't wait to tell you about this and knew you were supposed to get home from Stanford yesterday, so I called your mom and told her I had to see you ASAP. She said she didn't expect you until very late so not to look for you until morning. Thank heavens she sent you right over when you got up."

"Even without her prompting, I would have come on the double. I've missed you." Mindy blew a breath up her face, fluttering her bangs. "It was after one-thirty before I pulled in."

"I was still awake, so you could have come over."

Mindy blinked slowly. "I was so tired from the drive up from California, I couldn't keep my eyes open any longer."

Mar should be more tired than she was with how little sleep she'd gotten, but the adrenaline flowing through her veins was evidently sustaining her. She scooped up the pile of papers, books, and photos into her arms. "Let's take this into the living room where we'll have more space to spread it across the floor."

Mindy sat on the area rug with her. Mar re-examined the diaries, letters, and pictures one at a time, while her friend sifted through the documents and notes for any legal cues to see if Mar had missed a clue.

She started with the letters from her father to her mother.

She fingered the first envelope, postmarked 1968, over thirty years ago, more years than Mar was old. "I feel as though I barely knew him. I've lived twice as many years without him as with him."

"I scarcely knew him." Mindy shuffled the documents in front of her. "He was either working or we were at my house. But the few memories I do have, I remember he was always so nice to me."

Mar ran her thumb across her mother's maiden name in parentheses followed by Ross. The handwriting, though a little hard to read, seemed deliberate in its making. In it, he wrote how he missed her mom.

My Dearest Beth,

I know you are wondering where I am and what the weather is like here and if I'm staying warm and dry. I can tell you none of that. We were given a list of topics we couldn't include in our letters, and all of the above was on it and more. Our letters are read before they are approved to be mailed in case they get intercepted. If I mention anything I shouldn't, you'll know by the blackout marks. So, if you see any, you'll know I wrote something I shouldn't. But it obviously wasn't that important, so don't fret over it. Just know I'm doing all right and will return to you as soon as I can.

With little else to write about, I'll write of my love for you. It is both a blessing and a curse. Thinking of you gets me through the worst of days, but it also makes me ache to be with you all the more. There isn't a minute that goes by I don't think of your smiling face, laughing eyes, and soft lips. Oh, that I could kiss them now.

I try to live my life without regrets, but I have one now. My one regret is that we weren't able to tie the knot before I shipped out. Please forgive me for that. But no matter. You are still my wife. In my heart. In my head. And in every way that matters. When I return, we'll make it official, for no one can tear us apart.

I dream of you every night. My last thought before I fall asleep is of you. My first thought when I wake is of you. In between, I focus on staying alive so I can return home to you. You are my morning sun. You are my moon to light my way through this darkness.

My tour of duty is only two years, and it will fly by. Then I'll have you in my arms once again, and we can forge into the future, creating our life together over the next 100 years.

I must close now because it's time for chow. I'm ever looking forward to rushing back to you.

All my love is for you.

Your ever-devoted husband,

George

Mar took a quick breath. *Wow!* She had never imagined Dad had been that sentimental. Hopefully one day, Mar would find someone as romantic.

Mindy had moved on to one of the diaries.

More letters followed. *Hmm.* It didn't seem as though Dad knew about Mom's pregnancy. Though Mar put her parents' correspondence in order by date so they were all in one pile, the pieces didn't fit. "This doesn't make sense."

"What?" Mindy glanced up from the diary.

"It's like they are each ignoring what the other wrote. Mom told him that she was pregnant, but Dad said nothing about it." Mar shook her head. "I'll keep reading to see if it makes sense at any point." It soon became clear what had happened. "Oh, listen to this.

'My Dearest Beth,

Mail call is awful lonesome. It has been weeks, and I haven't received any news from you. I will chalk it up to the mail being ever so slow. Because the alternative, that your love for me has waned in my short absence, is too heavy of a burden to bear.'"

Mar clutched the letter to her chest. "How awful for him to believe Mom didn't love him anymore."

"It must have been so difficult for your parents."

Mar held back tears but nodded. They had been younger than she was now.

Mom's words became similarly despondent in tone until she'd received a whole batch of letters at once and expressed her joy at the surprise, stating she had laughed and cried at the same time.

Mar found herself in a similar state with tears of joy.

Her mother explained how she didn't have a mailing address and prayed daily to receive word from him. Curiously, the date of that mail delivery was thirty years ago this coming Christmas Eve. She missed them both.

Mindy held out the diary she was reading. "This is the entry where your mom suspects she's pregnant and goes to her mother's old doctor. Dr. Thomas told her the child would be born in June—that would be you—and said both she and the baby were doing fine. She also writes that he believes to have heard two heartbeats, so he ordered an ultrasound, then later called to tell her she was expecting twins."

Mar pulled one of the letters from the stack. "Here's the letter where Mom was so happy to give Dad his Christmas present—the news of their impending parenthood, me and my brother or sister." She locked her gaze on her friend. "I'm so glad I have you to help me through all this."

"I'm glad I'm here to do whatever I can." Mindy sipped her hot chocolate. "Let's do some supposing. We'll try to think like each of the people involved in your little drama and do some what-ifs. Once we have the most likely scenarios, we'll have somewhere to begin. Just like sorting out a court case. Determining the motives of each suspect is usually the best course."

After several rounds of speculating and getting nowhere, Mindy leaned back against the front of the couch. "I forgot to tell you, Mar—what with all the excitement. One of the lawyers at the firm I clerk for part-time in San Francisco wants to learn to ski. He's up visiting his sister and her family in Kirkland for the holidays. I told him we would have lunch with him to make plans. I thought we would take him under our wing and show him the best spots to hit the slopes."

"Oh, Mindy, you know we don't have any extra time. I was really hoping you could help me through this. There is so much to do and track down. You'll only be home for two weeks."

"Twelve days to be exact, before I head back, and we have Christmas and New Years to contend with. Over the holidays is a terrible time to be digging into something like this. But, Mar, he's the one who's been helping me get ready for the bar exam. He doesn't know anyone here except his sister. Can't we at least have lunch at the market? We need to eat somewhere anyhow, and we can tell him about this problem. To figure this all out, we might need a real lawyer to procure additional information and documentation, and I don't have my degree yet." Mindy pressed her palms together, nestled them up to her cheek, and pushed out her bottom lip.

"Don't beg." Mar sighed. "If you feel so strongly about it, we'll have lunch with him. Is there more to this than you've told me? Are you interested in this guy?"

Mindy straightened immediately. "Of course not. He's only a friend helping me study. Like a big brother. He has a vested interest. If I pass the bar—"

"When." Mar gave her friend a hard look.

"*When* I pass the bar, the company *might* make my position permanent, which will reduce his caseload, or at least reduce the number of his menial tasks, which would fall to me."

"Oh, Mindy, you aren't planning to stay in California, are you? I had hoped you would move back up here."

"I hope so too, but I may need to remain there for a few months to get things in order to take the bar up here as well. But that's a discussion for another day." Mindy waved her arms over the chaos on the floor. "I didn't know any of this when I talked to him before. I can explain we won't have time for skiing. I'm sure he'll assist us with your problem. He's really helpful and smart."

"What makes you think I want to tell my family's dark secrets to a stranger?" Mar's insides twisted at the thought.

"Don't be upset. I'm sure you'll be telling it to plenty of strangers before we get to the bottom of this." Mindy's expression turned more compassionate. "If you want answers, you can't keep this to yourself. I think you're tired and hungry. With less than two weeks off, we'll need to play it by ear anyhow. I'm convinced we'll need a lawyer before this is over, and Ken could be a big asset to our investigation and save us money at the same time."

Mar nodded, having settled down a bit and getting used to the idea of the whole world knowing—eventually. She also liked that her friend had automatically included herself as part of this.

Mindy always seemed to know what to say, too bad she got home only a few times a year. She had put her life on hold until next summer when she would graduate and take the bar exam.

Mindy pulled an eager expression. "So, shall I call Ken to have him meet us for lunch?"

Mar's stomach rumbled in response.

Mindy grinned. "I'll take that as a yes."

Mar nodded once again.

Mindy dashed to the phone in the kitchen.

This would give Mar a chance to see if this Ken fellow was good enough for her best friend.

Chapter Two

After Mindy's phone call, which took longer than needed, she returned. "He'll meet us at the entrance to Pike's Place Market at twelve-thirty."

Mar pinned Mindy with her gaze. "Tell me about Ken. Is it serious?"

Laughing, Mindy shook her head. "I told you, we're just friends. He's a really nice guy and fun to be with. I've promised to teach him how to become a northwest person. You know, like walking in the rain, riding ferry boats, and drinking lattes. So, we'll meet him at the market, eat crab sandwiches and Caesar salad. I always miss that when I'm off at school. I need someone to do things with once in a while, and Ken has fit the bill quite well."

"Okay." *Oh, there is more to their relationship than friendship.* At least on Mindy's end of things. "I get the picture. I realize you need to do things with someone else while I'm here slaving away, trying to earn enough to start my own agency. I haven't found anyone like that yet, so I just go down to the bookstore at the market alone. Grimaldi's is perfect now that they have an espresso machine." She downed the dregs of her cold hot chocolate.

Mindy rubbed her hands together. "Okay then. Let's get organized so we know what we're going to do the rest of the day. Besides lunch with Ken."

"Good idea." Mar straightened the heap of letters, then the journals, and lastly the documents. "The piles are tidied, but the information in them is all over the place."

Mindy bit her bottom lip. "Do you have any spiral notebooks and pens handy?"

Nodding, Mar crossed to the small desk and retrieved two slightly used notebooks from a lower drawer. Then she grabbed the cup of pens and pencils from the top and set them all on the coffee table. "I don't know which ones work, so I brought them all." She sat back on the floor where she had been before. "Now what?"

"Let's make a list of what we need to do. Then we can go through everything making lists of events."

Mar tapped her index finger on her lips. "Should I try to talk to Mrs. Thomas again? She may have remembered something. I could take a present to her at the nursing home. She might like that, and it could make her more willing to speak to me."

"That's a good idea, but let's see what we have to work with first. You don't want to go too soon or the nursing home staff might think you're pestering her." Mindy wrote in her notebook. "Before we forge ahead, we need to go through your mother's diaries and all the letters, recording everything that happened in chronological order. At the same time, we can list everyone involved so we can try to find them if we need more help."

Mindy discussed what information would be most helpful, while Mar wrote down questions.

Halting, Mar tapped her pen on the notebook in front of her. "I really need to talk to that new doctor in person, but his nurse was so hostile toward me. Another encounter with her will probably be just as unproductive as well as unpleasant."

Mindy shook her head. "You deal with disagreeable people every day at work. Why would you let some snippy young nurse intimidate you? You'll think of a way to get past her to talk to the doctor."

"You're right." Mar squared her shoulders. "I do know how to deal with those kinds of people. I guess this is just so important to me, I lost sight of reality for a moment. I'll try to get things back into perspective." She glanced at her watch. "It's noon already. We'd better get in gear if we're going to meet your friend. We only have half an hour, and you know how parking is around the market." Mar handed Mindy her jacket, then swung on her own before chasing her friend out the door.

Mindy tossed her car keys in the air and caught them. "We'll take my car. You drive like your mother in that old BMW." Then she twisted her mouth to the side. "You should, I guess, it was her car for a long time, and it's sure better than the ancient Bug you had in high school and college."

After jumping in Mindy's three-year-old red and gray Chevy Blazer, her friend drove toward downtown Seattle and their lunch date with Ken. Soon Mindy turned onto Pike Street.

Mar tapped her wristwatch. "We're nearly ten minutes late. Pull into one of the old brick parking garages. I'll pay."

Obeying without hesitation, Mindy made a hard left into the structure. After parking and emerging on the corner of Fifth and Pike, Mindy dashed diagonally across the street. Now on the market side, Mindy forged a path among the people coming and going.

Mar easily followed in her wake. *My goodness, Mindy's in more of a hurry than she needs to be.* Almost out of breath, Mar stopped at the entrance.

Mindy ran up to a tall, blond, relaxed-looking man leaning against one of the many paper and magazine racks near the sidewalk.

Smiling, he gave Mindy a hug and turned to Mar. "Hi. You must be the infamous Mar I've heard so much about. I'm Ken Austen."

"Guilty as charged." For some reason, she felt a rush of relief. How could a simple greeting from this calm, agreeable fellow have such an effect? "I'm pleased to meet the novel Ken I've heard so *little* about."

He raised an eyebrow.

Mar pulled a face. "Sorry. My attempt at humor. It sounded better in my head." She pointed to her temple.

He lifted his chin in understanding. "I take it Mindy hasn't mentioned me before."

"You, sir, are a well-guarded secret."

"Hey." Mindy held up her hands. "I haven't exactly been home long enough to mention him, let alone say much about him. You kept me kind of busy all morning." Mindy shook her head. "Oh, you two. I can tell you're like peas in a pod, and I'll likely regret ever introducing the pair of you. Come on. I'm starving." Linking arms with Ken and Mar, she wound her way through the milling crowds down the walkway among the buckets of fresh flowers and seafood stands to the Greek Café. Settling in a booth overlooking the ferry terminal, Mindy let out a sigh of what appeared to be sheer happiness.

Studying her friend across the table, Mar laughed. "What are you so smug about?"

"Who, me?" Mindy put on an innocent expression. "Just happy to be with my two best friends in one of my favorite places. Wouldn't that please anybody?"

Ken glanced from Mindy to Mar and back. "I already know Mindy's terrific, and I can tell that the both of you together are going to be fun to hang around with. What do we do next?"

Mar laughed and Mindy joined her, but before either could answer, the waiter appeared.

Ari waved his pen at them. "If I know these two, they're going to make you eat crab sandwiches and Caesar salad. The only question I need answered is do you want one shot of espresso or two in your latte?"

Ken's blue eyes widened, and he chuckled. "You might as well give me whatever they're having. It seems they already have control of the situation."

"You got it." Ari tapped his pad and went off to place the order, reappearing soon with a trio of ice waters. Setting the glasses on the table, he leaned toward Mindy. "How's law school going?"

She gave a pained expression and moaned. "It's brutal, but fortunately, I have this guy as my mentor." She motioned toward Ken. "It's up to him to see that I get my degree and pass the bar exam, so be especially nice to him. I've been bragging about this place and what great food we have in the northwest. You won't let me down, will you?"

"Of course not." Ari turned to Ken. "Where are you from that you don't know about our food?"

"I'm originally from Indiana, but after I graduated from UCLA Law, I received a good offer from a firm in the Bay Area, and that's where I am now. Mindy works as a law clerk in our firm until she finishes at Stanford."

"Ken has a sister in Kirkland," Mindy volunteered, "and decided to come for the holidays so he could see the Pacific Northwest for himself I'm always raving about."

Glancing around, Ari inclined his head. "Looks like your order's ready. Let me grab that for you." He quickly returned, placing a large bowl of salad and a plate of sandwiches on the table. "I'll be right back with the lattes." In short order, he reappeared carrying a tray with the beverages and plates for the family-style dining. Smiling broadly, he gave a sharp salute. "Enjoy."

Mindy trained her gaze on Ken. "You'll love these crab sandwiches better than the ones in California." She turned her attention to Mar. "Sometimes on weekends, we're worn out from my studies, so we drive down to Fisherman's Wharf for fresh crab and clam chowder. It's as close as I can get to home."

Mar was stumped for words. Not because of anything Mindy said, but because of what she didn't say. Just friends? Ken her big brother? Hardly. The way her friend talked, one would think Mindy and Ken had been dating for years.

And then there was the manner in which Ken gazed at Mindy. Mar's heart broke a little. Her best friend was going to move on to the next phase of her life, get married, have children, and leave Mar behind. She wished this pair all the best if Mindy would ever acknowledge her feelings for this guy.

Digging into the food with relish, the three of them ate in silence. Soon the plates sat empty. With a sigh, Mar settled back to finish her latte. Mindy mimicked her action.

Ken leaned forward. "I hate to admit this, but I think you were right about the food. How will I ever go back to the Wharf's crab? I hope the rest of the holidays will be as good as today."

Mindy set her empty cup down. "That's the plan, but we won't be able to go skiing." She shifted her attention to Mar. "You've been awfully quiet for a long time. Is there a problem we should know about?"

Having been friends for two and a half decades, Mar knew Mindy's unspoken words. "I'm fine with taking time away for lunch. The break has been good." She sighed contently. "I'm just relaxing."

Ken furrowed his brow quizzically.

Mar nodded toward Ken. "Oh, there's something you should know. Mindy and I can read each other's minds."

"Can you now?" His mouth curved in a half-smile.

Mindy leaned forward. "What am I thinking now?"

Mar leaned forward as well until she was a few inches from Mindy's face. "You want to know what I think of your *Ken*—I mean your friend. Will I accept or reject him as a member of our party?"

Ken gazed at Mar with an expectant expression.

She tried to keep her focus on Mindy who appeared about ready to leap across the table and force an answer. Oh, yah, her friend liked this guy more than she was ready to admit. "I feel very comfortable with Ken. I hope he feels the same about me. I never expected to be this at ease with him so soon." The poor guy should be commended for putting up with the pair of them.

Mindy tilted her head. "Does that mean you want him to join us for the rest of the day on your quest or not?"

Ken cleared his throat. "Please don't feel obligated."

Mar gave him a nod. "I don't, but we still have lots to accomplish today. Are you sure you want to tag along? It might be boring for you."

Ken gave a half-shrug. "I'm game."

The man didn't even know what he was in for. However, his involvement would give Mar a good indication of his worthiness of her best friend.

"Well then, let's get on with it." Mar swigged the last of her latte. "We can fill you in, Ken, on what I'm up against as we go." Sliding out of the booth, she waved to Ari for the check.

Smiling, he waved back. "Today's on me. Merry Christmas."

Blowing kisses, Mar went out the double glass doors with Mindy at her side.

Ken gave Ari the same salute he had given them earlier and backed out the doors.

Mar and her friends became part of a milling mass of people surrounded by every imaginable kind of seafood, fruit, vegetable, flower, and fragrant baked good. It had been too long since she'd been down here. Unfortunately, today was not a day to linger.

Ken turned to Mindy. "I've never seen any place like this. In fact, I've never even heard of a place like this."

"That's because there isn't any place like this. This *is* the place." She gasped and widened her eyes. "I forgot to ask how you got here. Did you bring a vehicle or were you dropped off?"

He smiled at her concern. "My brother-in-law dropped me off and went back to his office. I'm supposed to call if I need him to pick me up or anything."

"Okay. Let's go to the car. You can call from my house and tell him not to wait for you. We'll take you home when we're through with you. I mean when we're finished explaining tonight." Mar motioned toward the exit.

Mindy shrugged. "Sorry, Ken. There wasn't time to prepare you for Mar's conundrum because it came to light just this morning. And it really is her story to tell. I suppose neither of us is much more comfortable with it than we expect you to be."

Mar led the way out of the structure, then dodged traffic, crossing streets to the Blazer. She had mixed feelings about bringing Ken—a relative stranger—in on her personal family mystery. She had contemplated not even telling Mindy but rather investigating this all on her own. That way, if she failed, she could blame it on not having help, and therefore she would still have hope. However, with two other people working on this—smart people—if she failed then her hope would be crushed.

Too late to change her mind now. Mindy knew, and Ken had been teased with potential intrigue. She had to believe, between the three of them, her dream of finding out about her sibling would come true.

Chapter Three

Though not yet three o'clock when Mindy pulled her Chevy into Mar's driveway, the fast-approaching sunset nudged closer and closer to the horizon on this gray day. Piling into the entryway off the back porch, Mar and her friends shrugged off their outer clothing and went into the warm, cheery kitchen.

Mindy waved her hand toward the table. "Make yourself comfortable, Ken, while Mar prepares hot chocolate." She left and returned a moment later with her arms full of the letters, journals, and documents.

Mar joined the other two at the table with three steaming mugs of chocolate goodness. Ready or not, the secrets from her past were about to be spilled, like dumping out a 5,000-piece puzzle. She took a deep breath, then related the story of her discovery and the mystery of the other baby.

Ken remained silent like a member of a jury prepared to pass judgment.

She ached to know what he was thinking. Mindy—as her best friend—sort of had to side with her. But did this attorney, who specialized in facts, think her crazy? Would he deem her ramblings the fantasies of a young woman desperate to cling to the smallest thread of her mother? Searching for some connection—any connection? Mar had to admit she longed for one.

Ken pushed back his chair. "You might be right about the disappearance of the other child. There doesn't seem to be any proof your twin did indeed die. But mind you, there also is no proof there *was* a second baby." He picked up Mar's birth certificate. "This indicates that you were a single birth."

Mar widened her eyes. *No, don't steal this from me so quickly.* "But what about Mom's diaries, and Dr. Thomas hearing two heartbeats *and seeing* twins on the ultrasound?"

"That's what's puzzling. Diaries, journals, letters, and other things put down in writing most often hold up in a court of law as factual. So, if there was a second baby, it may be that Dr. and Mrs. Thomas didn't note it so they could sell the child, which would help cover their costs from not charging your mother."

Mar gasped, and her hand flew to her throat. "Oh, I don't think the Thomases would do anything like that. They were kind people." At least from what she remembered as a child. The disturbing idea of her sibling being sold sent a shiver wriggling down her spine and twisted her gut.

Ken gave her a sympathetic look. "We can't rule anything out until we have proof either way. Another possibility is they knew a couple who wanted a baby and felt they were doing both your mother and the other couple a favor. They may have believed your parents, or your mother being alone, wouldn't be able to support or even physically care for two infants at once."

Mar didn't like that scenario any more than her brother or sister being sold, but it did sit a little better.

Ken went on. "Likewise, we can't rule out that the baby did die. Dr. Thomas could have thought listing you as a single birth was kinder to your mother so she wouldn't feel the loss. She had enough to deal with while your father was fighting in Vietnam. A lot of men didn't return from that war. Or your mom could have imagined she was having two babies. Truly believing it. She seemed to be under a lot of stress."

Mar chose to believe in a twin rather than Mom being completely wrong and imagining things. Her mother had never had the propensity for wild flights of fancy. "If my sibling did pass away, how will I ever know?"

"We should be able to find proof in the county files. Even though Christmas is at the end of the week, the courthouse should be open tomorrow with minimal staff. I'll go check birth and death records for the year you were born. Though I hold a California license, I might be able to get some answers."

What a relief. Mar hadn't realized she had placed so much hope in him being able to help. "I'm glad to hear you say that. I must confess, I was beginning to wonder if I've read more into this story than there actually is. What do you suggest I do about visiting Mrs. Thomas at the nursing home?"

"There shouldn't be any problem with that, but let's see what we can find first." Ken picked up her mother's birth certificate, holding it next to Mar's. He set the pair of documents in the center of the table. "Did you know that Dr. Thomas also delivered your mother?"

Mar picked them up. Dr. Thomas's name was on both. "I never knew that."

Ken nodded. "It's curious for sure. It could be very helpful to have a copy of your mother's medical records. You are planning to see the doctor who took over Dr. Thomas's practice, aren't you?"

"I keep telling myself I have to do that, but the experience I had this morning with the office nurse, Patty, has left a bad taste in my mouth. I'm just not ready to deal with her again. Mindy advised me to handle her in the same manner I do with other difficult people, and I will. It seems harder than most experiences I've had, probably because this is personal, and I need to find answers so badly."

Mindy put her hand on Mar's forearm. "Mar doesn't have any real family left since her mom died over a year ago. I'm as close to her as anyone could be, but having a flesh and blood sibling would probably be like getting someone of her own back. Her grandparents died before she was born and her father perished in a plane crash when she was ten."

Ken's courtroom business expression softened to something akin to compassion. "I'll do what I can to find your sibling if there is one, but I make no promises."

Mar didn't expect any. "I'm grateful for any help you can give me."

"Let's hold off on visiting that doctor and see what we can come up with at the courthouse. If we are armed with evidence of foul play, he might be more cooperative."

"So, what do we do now?" Mar was so glad to have others help carry her burden.

Mindy put her hand on one of the spiral notebooks. "Before we met you for lunch, we had started to go through some of this stuff and make lists of what we were finding."

He gifted her with a smile. "A wise course of action, counselor. If one of you will give me a few sheets of paper and tell me which items you want me to tackle, I'll assist with those lists."

"Divide and conquer." Mindy quickly tore out several pages and handed them to him.

Mar couldn't believe he was so eager to help. Was it the mystery that drew him in? The legal dilemma? Or a certain blond law student? She picked up one of the diaries for herself. "I've already read the letters for a third or fourth time—I've lost count—so if one of you wants to have a go at them to see if you pick up something I didn't."

Mindy raised her hand. "I'll do that."

Ken gave a nod. "Then I'll take this diary after I read through the legal documents more thoroughly."

A couple of hours later, Mindy stretched her arms above her head and arched her back. "I don't know about you two, but I'm starving. Let's order a pizza and see if we can formulate a game plan for this search. Remember, we have less than two weeks off, that's only ten business days, 'til we have to be back in California for work and classes. But we also have Christmas and New Years in there that cut down our time."

Nodding, Mar stood. "What kind of pizza do you like, Ken?"

Mindy chimed in. "Mar and I usually have Canadian bacon with pineapple from Godfathers."

Ken lifted his chin. "That sounds good."

Mar feared he was merely agreeing with Mindy because he liked her. "With three of us, we'll need two. Your choice, Ken."

"What about an all-meat combo?"

"Mmm. I haven't had one of those in a long time." Mar's stomach growled softly in agreement as she crossed to the phone and ordered.

Mindy laid her hands flat on the table. "Shall we clear this off or eat in the living room?"

"Living room. It will be nice to take a short break." Though Mar wished she didn't have to stop to eat at all. She felt as though she were cramming for a final exam she had no knowledge of until the night before. So much to learn.

Twenty-five minutes later, the doorbell rang.

With excitement, Mar faced her best friend who sported the same eager expression, then jumped to her feet and raced to the entryway with Mindy on her heels. She threw open the door, startling the pizza delivery boy. Giggling, Mindy took the boxes with the divine aroma.

Mar dug into her purse.

From behind her, Ken said, "I'll get this."

Mar waved him off. "Oh, no you don't. Not only are you my guest, but you're helping me. Consider this pay for services rendered."

With a huff of breath, he backed off.

By the time she returned to the living room, Mindy had plunked herself on the floor, one box lid already flung open on the coffee table, and a slice of fruity pizza in hand.

Sitting on the floor as well, Mar took a piece of their usual and bit off a huge chunk, continuing the small talk around the food in her mouth.

Ken, apparently being more proper, sat on the couch. He held an all-meat combo wedge in his hand.

After the trio polished off most of the pizza, Mar combined the remaining slices into one box, carried it into the kitchen, and popped it into the fridge. The other two followed and settled themselves at the table.

Ken pulled the sheets of paper he'd been writing on toward himself. "Let's compare lists. Probably the names that appear most often on all three are the ones we need to trace first."

"Look here." Mar pointed. "We all wrote Paul and Rose Swanson several times. I vaguely remember Mom and Dad talking about them, long ago. I don't think they live around here now, though. I remember reading they had moved to eastern Washington years ago."

Mindy squealed. "Oo. I read in my batch she was your mother's matron-of-honor. You must have been about two then. I'm positive they were your parents' closest friends in those days."

"Undoubtedly." Ken tapped the marriage certificates. "Paul and Rose Swanson signed as witnesses at your parents' real wedding, and they were also listed as the witnesses on the original license but as Paul Swanson and Rose Bjornson."

Mar drew in a deep breath. Things were coming together. She might actually get answers. "Now that we've decided whom to look for, how do we go about it? Hire a detective? Or maybe do it ourselves just as quickly?"

Ken thought for a moment. "An ad in the Seattle newspaper might be the best course of action. Do people in eastern Washington read it?"

"They do. That's a good idea." Mar's hopes continued to climb. "Even if they don't get it themselves, someone who knows them might call either us or the Swansons."

Mindy poised her pencil over the spiral notebook in front of her. "Let's figure out how we want it to read, and we can contact the newspaper in the morning. We have two here, but if it's put in one, it prints in both of them. How long do we want to run it?"

After a few moments of silence, Ken responded. "My initial inclination would be a week, but with the holidays, let's start with two weeks. If you don't get a response in that length of time, you can extend it. One more thing, Mar, if we haven't found them by the time schools are in session again, you could check with their old high school and colleges to see if the alumni lists have their address."

"Say, Mar?" Mindy pointed her pencil at her best friend. "Did you see any pictures of the Swansons in those old photos? Maybe one from the wedding. Let's see what they look like."

"I can't remember. It's all a jumble after learning so much in such a short amount of time and going through all this stuff over and over. I'll get them." Mar retrieved the stack from the coffee table in the living room. The built-in oak bookcases on either side of the fireplace caught her attention. All the family albums and school annuals were stored on the bottom shelf. "Guys, come here."

Both Ken and Mindy appeared, and Mindy spoke. "Did you find something?"

"Boy, did I." Mar pulled out four annuals and handed them to Ken. "These are my parents' yearbooks." She grabbed an equal number of photo albums, giving two to Mindy and keeping a couple for herself. Then she scooped up the pile of pictures she had originally come for. "Let's take these to the kitchen."

Mindy set the books on the table. "Where do we start?"

"I'll go through the photographs. Would you two tackle the yearbooks?" None of the snapshots had any identification. The only ones of the wedding just had Mom and Dad in them. Sighing, Mar set them aside. "Nothing. I hope you two are having better luck."

Ken straightened and tapped a page. "Here's your dad's basketball team. It says this is Paul Swanson standing next to him."

Mindy and Mar crowded closer.

Ken pushed the leather-covered volume in front of them. "I'll see if I can find Beth and Rose in one of these other yearbooks."

Mar studied the pair. Her dad was a few inches taller, but both were handsome guys. She turned page after page, then stopped suddenly. "Here's Mom and a short girl named Rose on the staff of both the school paper and the yearbook. I'll bet she's the Rose we're searching for. Let's locate them in all the yearbooks and see if we can learn more about them." She carefully scanned each page and wrote down the picture titles and page numbers of those she found. Her friends did the same.

After nearly an hour of silence, Mindy raised her head. "Rose was a short girl. Your mom wasn't very tall, but Rose is at least three inches shorter. She has such little bones and seems almost fragile. I saw her on top of the cheerleading pyramid."

"I found her on the pep squad their sophomore year, but then she became a cheerleader in her junior and senior years." Mar stretched her neck from one side to the other.

Mindy closed the annual in front of her. "Now that we know what they looked like, we can go through the albums and pictures again to see if we can find any more of them."

They all found several more photos.

Noticing her friends' droopy eyes, Mar stood. "We've made great progress. I think that's enough work for one day. We can get back to it again tomorrow. It's after eleven and time for us to take Mr. Attorney home."

Ken stood as well. "It's too late for you two to be driving me around. I'll call a cab, then see if I can rent a car tomorrow."

Mindy dug in her purse. "A rental is too expensive. I'm staying here at Mar's. Take my car." She dangled her keys in front of him.

He took them. "Are you sure?"

"Positive. Mar has a car if we need to get around."

Mar snagged the spare house key off a hook on the kitchen wall. "Take this. In case we're still asleep when you arrive. You can just come on in."

"Thanks."

Mindy walked Ken out.

Because she and Mindy spent so much time at each other's house growing up, they each had a permanent bed in their room for the other. Not ready to move on from her mom's passing, Mar had remained in the room she'd grown up in. Mindy could have slept in the spare room, but what kind of slumber party would that be?

Her thoughts tumbled back to her quandary.

A *twin*.

She had a twin!

Chapter Four

Mar woke to the aroma of fresh coffee at 8:30. Her fitful dreams had been fraught with her baby twin crying, but she hadn't been able to locate the infant. In one, she actually held the little one, but even in the dream, she knew it wasn't right. Her twin would be grown up.

Across the room nestled in the bed on the opposite wall, Mindy remained sound asleep. So, if she wasn't brewing coffee, who was?

Mar climbed out of bed and padded to the window. Sure enough, Mindy's Chevy sat parked in the driveway. That meant Ken had arrived.

After a speedy shower, Mar returned to the bedroom, dressing in a beige, black, and white bouclé sweater with beige slacks. On her way out, she gently shook her friend. "Time to wake up."

Mindy moaned.

Mar leaned closer and whispered in her ear. "I smell coffee."

"You already made coffee?" Her friend sniffed then sat up.

"Not me." Mar shook her head. "I haven't been in the kitchen yet, but I can guess who it might be. A certain handsome someone I gave a key to last night."

Mindy's mouth pulled into a wide smile. "Let me quick take a shower." She hustled across to the bathroom.

Down the hall and into the kitchen, Mar found exactly whom she expected. Not only had Ken made coffee, he'd gotten out different pans, chopped a variety of veggies—he must have brought with him—and set three places at the table. He'd obviously been here for a while. Now, he sat at the table reading her morning paper, The Post Intelligencer. Even with his tie loose and his dress shirt sleeves rolled up, he was still way overdressed for her kitchen.

Mar smiled at him. "Good morning. It appears you're planning quite a spread."

"Just crepes and omelets." Ken shrugged one shoulder. "I hope you don't mind that I made myself at home in your kitchen. I thought it would be fun to make breakfast for Mindy—and you."

Just crepes and omelets? That was a major breakfast. "I, for one, think it's great to wake up with a handsome chef in my kitchen, creating divine aromas. I told Mindy to rise and shine." She poured herself a mug of coffee and walked to the small bay window seat. "Apparently, Seattle's famous blue sky isn't going to show itself for you again today. But at least you won't have to contend with rain while you're driving around."

He crossed to her. "How can you tell? Don't clouds equal rain?"

"These aren't the get-you-all-wet kind. People think it rains all the time in Seattle, but it doesn't. Often cloudy though."

"I was surprised it was so cold. I had to scrape the windows of the Blazer this morning. I'm glad I trusted Mindy and dug out my winter coat before coming. Even so, I never imagined all the green that would be this far north at this time of year. It's so beautiful even with the clouds."

"Don't tell anyone, please. We wouldn't want people flocking here and crowding us out." Mar turned to face the kitchen. "Mindy should be along soon. Is there anything I can do to help with breakfast?"

"Everything's ready to go." Ken took up his position at the stove. "I'll start the crepes now, and when Mindy comes in, the omelets."

Before Ken had half-a-dozen crepes in the warming oven, Mindy entered wearing a pair of jeans and a U-Dub sweatshirt. She rubbed a towel on her still-damp hair. "Something sure smells good. I know Mar didn't do all this. I'll make a wild guess and give the credit to Ken."

Mar mentally shook her head. Her friend already knew it wasn't Mar, but Mindy had made a point of complimenting the man who was special in her life—even though she wouldn't admit it. Mar poured coffee into a fresh mug and handed it to Mindy.

Dropping her towel on the back of a chair, her friend cupped her hands around the warm ceramic and breathed in the roasted brew. "Mmm. Everything smells wonderful."

Ken gazed at Mindy with a satisfied grin. "What do you want in your omelet?"

Once they placed their orders, Ken cooked them up in a flash.

After eating more than she should, Mar sat back in her chair and patted her stomach. "Everything was delicious."

Mindy echoed the sentiment with an extra dose of praise. A little too much.

Ken stacked the plates and stood. "I suppose I'd better load the dishwasher, so I don't get a swollen head."

Mar gathered the stray silverware and used napkins. "We should do that. You did the cooking. Besides, you're heading off to the courthouse."

"All right." He retrieved his suit jacket from the back of his chair and swung it on.

Mar gave Ken the once over. "You're pretty spiffy in that blue suit."

Ken cinched up his striped tie, then added his winter dress coat. "I thought if I was going to the courthouse, they might pay more attention if I actually looked like a lawyer."

"Well, you will undoubtedly impress them." Mar scrunched her eyebrows, squinting. "Do you always bring a suit with you on vacation?"

Mindy glanced up, nodding. "I get so used to seeing him like that at work, I often forget how dressed up he is."

"You've been spending too much time with lawyers." Mar heaved a sigh.

Ken chuckled. "I thought I might need it for church, but my sister already nixed that. She said I would appear too uptight in it. But now it's going to come in handy." Ken picked up his briefcase. "I'm outta here. See you girls later—with news, I hope."

Mar pulled an exaggerated confused face. "Don't tell me you vacation with a briefcase too?"

He chuckled. "Unfortunately, my job demands it. Work never stops. I have a deposition to go over."

Mindy lifted her hand in a pseudo-wave. "Good luck." With that, Ken disappeared through the doorway.

Mar snatched her car keys off the hook on the wall. "We should head out too. Are you ready?"

Mindy pointed toward the sink. "What about the dishes? You told Ken we would take care of them."

"We'll do them when we get back." With that Mar headed outside and slid into the driver's seat of the BMW. Mindy got in on the passenger side. Mar drove toward downtown Seattle and the newspaper office. Past King Street Station and the international district, she wound through the traffic. Crossing rail and trolley tracks, passing various ferry terminals, waterfront restaurants, and finally the market itself, she perused for a parking place.

"Let's park in a waterfront lot near the Post-Intelligencer Building," Mindy suggested. "That way we'll have our choice of places to eat lunch."

Mar harrumphed. "No matter where either of us suggests, you know we'll end up at the market again, so why pretend any differently? And do you realize how far it is from here?"

"You know we eat at other places. Besides, you love it and you know it."

After parking, Mar, with Mindy at her side, entered the big newspaper building sporting the gigantic globe on its roof. Finding the information desk, she spoke to the young college student there. "Where do I go to place a personal ad?"

She pointed. "Down this hall and to the right."

"Thank you." She hurried that way with Mindy. "You have the piece of paper we used to plan out the ad, don't you?" She chuckled. "I should have asked you that *before* we left the house."

Her friend pulled a folded sheet of paper from her purse and waved it in the air. "I've got you covered."

The clerk at the ad desk was quite helpful. When finished and all paid up, Mar asked the young man, "We want to search some old newspapers. Where would we go to do that?"

"Anything more than a year old will be in the archives in the basement. Anything recent to a year, may or may not be on microfiche down there, but Carl will help you determine where they might be."

"Thanks." She and Mindy took the elevator to the lowest floor of the building. The long, barren hallway with several blank doors on each side led to one at the end titled Microfilm Library. Entering, Mar approached the thirty-something gentleman with thick glasses. "Are you Carl?"

He nodded. "How may I help you?"

"We would like to look at papers from June 1969."

"Are you searching for something specific in those editions? Or those papers as a whole?"

"Births and deaths mostly."

He waved toward a bank of microfiche machines. "Sit at any two you like, and I'll bring the films."

Less than ten minutes later, Carl set a stack of microfiche envelopes between the pair of readers. "Do you know how to operate these machines?"

Mar nodded.

Mindy sighed. "Intimately. I use them all the time at the law library."

"Fine. Let me know if you need anything else." Carl retreated to his desk.

Mar took a deep breath. And so began the search.

Of the births, Mar didn't find an announcement of her own or any similar to hers, but few people put an announcement in the paper. However, obituaries were plentiful. No infants matched her statistics. A boy, Daniel, born three days before her passed away on the day she came into the world. That couldn't be her twin. Another baby born a week and a half after her also didn't live. "This seems to be a dead end."

Mindy stood. "Let me get papers for when your parents' wedding took place."

"Good idea. Also, ask for the time they originally were going to get married."

With the new batch of films, still, nothing usable turned up.

Not knowing exactly what she was hunting for made the work frustrating.

"I've been sitting too long." Mar stood and twisted from side to side. "My legs are cramping. I could use a walk."

Mindy stretched her arms over her head. "I know we were thinking of eating closer, but a little exercise sounds good. We could hike down to our favorite lunch spot at the Market."

Mar laughed. "I told you this would happen. The run down may be good for us, but remember it's just about a mile back up the hill after we eat."

"We'll take it easy." Mindy hitched her purse over her shoulder.

The grade of the hill naturally sped up Mar's pace. She was at the bottom before she knew it.

Entering the market by the main door, Mar and Mindy moved carefully past the flowers, vegetables, and flying fish. Mar ducked and grinned with a wave at the fellows in white coats and knee-high rubber boots who entertained themselves and tourists by tossing the big fish from one area to another. After opening the door of the cafe, they entered and sat at the long, curved counter on stools.

Mar got up, hung their coats on the large metal coat rack, and, stepping over to the kitchen pass-through, called out to Mrs. Constanopoulos, "Is Ari busy?"

"He's not here today," she answered. "But Rosa and Gina both are. It's busy, busy back here, so I must stay in the kitchen. I'll send Rosa out."

Mar sat back at the counter. "What do you want to eat? We already had our regular yesterday with Ken."

Mindy perused the menu. "I'm tired of being good. Let's have chowder and antipasto."

"You call all that pizza we ate last night good?"

"Please?"

Mar sighed. With the family-style dining, they either needed to agree on a meal or have *way* too much food. "We'd better be careful. We'll want to go home and take a nap instead of searching the files some more."

Rosa approached and set glasses of ice water in front of them. "Hi, girls. I haven't seen both of you in here together for quite a while. I'm not usually here when you come in since having the baby."

Mar smiled. "I'm glad you're here today. How is little Matthew? Growing like a weed I suppose."

"Little?" She widened her eyes. "He's going to have to carry me around soon. He weighs almost thirty pounds already, and he's only sixteen months old." She sighed. "Now, what are you going to have? The usual?"

Mindy licked her lips. "No. Since we had that yesterday, we're going to expand a little. We'll have antipasto, calamari, clam chowder, and those wonderful hard rolls."

"Okay." Rosa left, hung the order, and returned with the cups of chowder. "You want lattes?"

Mar shook her head. "I think I'll stick with water."

"Me too." Mindy nodded.

Rosa collected an order from the pass-through and strolled off into the dining room to deliver it.

"Calamari *and* rolls? You're going to be sleeping at that microfiche machine this afternoon rather than helping me."

"I promise not to nap until we get back to your house." Mindy made an X on her chest.

Soon, Rosa served them their food, and Mar dug in, enjoying the antipasto and calamari more than she should. She would start being good tomorrow. She mentally shook her head. Who was she kidding? The holidays would make that impossible. January first then.

Mindy tore a roll in two and pointed one half at Mar. "I've been thinking about the way we're approaching this, and I wonder if we shouldn't find Dr. Thomas's obituary in the newspaper files. I'd like to see what relatives are listed. They might give us a clue about names to look under. It'll also tell what funeral home handled everything. Do you suppose they might have a copy of who was there and who was financially responsible?"

"Mindy, that's a wonderful idea. That could save us a lot of digging through old articles and birth statistics. You're going to be one terrific lawyer. Think about it, you'll get paid for sitting around thinking up these kinds of questions."

"Well, I hope so, that's the whole idea of killing myself studying."

After every last bit of food was consumed, Mar motioned toward the empty dishes. "One would think we hadn't eaten a huge gourmet breakfast this morning."

Mindy patted her stomach, much like Mar had done at breakfast. "I'm making up for lost meals while studying, and I need to stock up for the coming lean days. What's your excuse?'"

"My only excuse is I have a weakness for good food." Mar paid and stood. "Time to work off some of this on the trek back up the steep hill. There be files awaiting."

As Mindy stood, she yawned.

Mar shook her finger. "Oh, no you don't. You promised."

Mindy covered her mouth. "I'll stay awake. I won't even blink."

Outside, the sharply cold air fanned by a brisk breeze from the water revitalized Mar. She hadn't even realized she'd been sinking into a lethargy from the large lunch. "The crisp air ought to wake you up."

Mindy drew in a deep breath. "Wide awake and raring to go."

The sidewalk sloped up, then leveled out mostly, looking directly over Elliot Bay where boats came and went. The return trip to the Post-Intelligencer Building took much longer than the run down, just over twenty minutes.

Back in the microfilm library, Mar asked Carl for newspapers around the time of Dr. Thomas's death. Once she found his obituary, she requested a photocopy of it. "I don't know what else we can learn here. Shall we head back to my house?"

Mindy scanned the obit. "He was buried at West Seattle Cemetery, and Brower's Funeral Home made the arrangements. It's not out of our way, and we may get more help if we stop there in person than if we call. What do you say?"

"Excellent plan. I hope Ken is having better luck than us."

"I'm sure he is. We'll compare the names in this article and whatever information we collect at the funeral home and cemetery, then go over everything with Ken and what he found."

Mar climbed into her car as did Mindy. "I can't wait for my personal ad to come out. It's amazing that it will be in tomorrow's paper because of computers. We squeezed in just under the deadline."

"I don't think we did." Mindy shook her head. "But that clerk sure thought you were cute. He was so flirting with you. I'm surprised he didn't ask for your phone number."

Mar gave a tight smile. "I had to put it on the form."

Mindy opened her mouth wide. "Ah. He is *so* calling you."

"I doubt that. The only person I want to call is Rose or Paul Swanson or someone who knows them. I suppose that's too much to hope for on the first day of the ad, though."

The assistant director at Brower's Funeral Home was a woman in her late thirties who remembered the Thomas funeral well.

Mar forged ahead. "As a family friend, I'm following up to make sure all the finances have been taken care of satisfactorily." Not a lie. She did know the doctor and his wife.

"I believe that file is closed, so that would mean there is nothing outstanding. Let me double-check." The woman fingered through a file folder from a desk drawer labeled *Invoices*. "Yes. The Thomases' niece took care of all the transactions promptly. Mrs. Gordon was such a nice lady."

Mrs. Gordon. Mar made a mental note of the name. "Do you have a current address for her? I would like to write and thank her."

Mrs. Jensen scrolled the address on a piece of paper. "I'm sure she would appreciate hearing from you. It helps the grieving cope with death when they receive kind words from people, even ones they haven't heard from in a while."

"Thank you so much." Mar slipped the paper into her purse without looking at it. "One more thing. I'm trying to put together a family genealogy chart of sorts. Would it be possible to get a list of people who attended the funeral?"

"Genealogies can be so challenging, especially finding all the names needed to trace everyone. I've run into several immovable roadblocks in my own search, but I won't give up. That information would be filed in the other room. I'll be right back." Mrs. Jensen slipped out through a side door.

Mindy bumped Mar with her shoulder. "Genealogy? That was smart."

"It seems as though everyone is tracing their genealogy these days. Fellow seekers like to help each other."

"What if she hadn't been and said no?"

"I would have thanked her and left."

Mrs. Jensen returned with a pair of folded papers. "These are a copy of the guest book. The head of the funeral home likes to keep a photocopy in case the police need it. He's such a conspiracy theorist. I've blacked out the personal information like addresses and phone numbers."

Mar took the papers. "I totally understand. The names will be a tremendous help. Thank you so much."

"Good luck with building your family tree."

Mar waved as she exited.

Mindy stuck close to Mar. "She was really nice. When I die, I want her to take care of my funeral."

"Do you think she'll still be working here in fifty or sixty years?"

Mindy twisted her mouth to the side. "Good point."

Mar got in and started the car. "I want to visit his gravesite. See if his marker has any useful information."

"I can't imagine it would, but it's on the way."

A little bit later, Mar read the inlaid grave markers as she wound her way through the cemetery to find the right one. Mrs. Patricia Ellington lived to the ripe old age of ninety-six. Henry Peabody had only been middle-aged. And one for a *Baby G*. Mar pointed. "Ah. There it is." She stood, staring at the recessed plaque in the ground. Next to it, one waited for Mrs. Thomas.

Mindy heaved a sigh. "See. Nothing useful."

Mar read aloud. "'Loving husband and son.'"

"So?"

"So, it doesn't say Father, which means they had no children. That's sad." It must have been lonely in his old age.

After a moment of silence, Mindy spoke up. "Let's go home and sort through what we got."

The drive didn't take long, and Mar parked in front of the house, leaving the driveway clear for Ken and the Chevy. Even before they entered the house, he pulled in and got out.

Ken's expression clearly declared he hadn't made any remarkable progress. "Today was discouraging."

Mindy faced him. "Don't feel bad. We might have found some information that'll put us on a better trail."

Mar unlocked the door. "Let's go inside and warm up first."

Rosy-cheeked from the cold, Mar and her friends shuffled in, pulling off jackets and gloves.

Mar pointed toward the living room. "I'm going to check phone messages."

Mindy crossed to the stove. "I'll start the hot chocolate."

Mar glanced at the answering machine. The indicator light wasn't blinking. No messages. Why should there be? The ad hadn't even come out yet.

Armed with Dr. Thomas's obit, Mrs. Gordon's address, and the list of funeral attendees, Mar sat at the table with the others. Excited by the realization of possibly being on the right track, she relayed all she and Mindy had discovered. "We need to compare what we found today with the information my mom left to see if there are any matches."

"You ladies had better luck than me. Maybe you two should go to the courthouse."

That was disappointing. Mar had hoped Ken would come back with the birth certificate she needed. Even a death certificate would have told her something. "Anything remotely close?"

"Nothing in the correct time frame. I found birth and death certificates for a boy born three days before you and passed away on your birthday."

"We found Daniel in the paper as well. Since the courthouse was a bust, what do we do now? I don't understand how they can have no information on a person born in the late sixties. It's not like it was the Dark Ages, and you could hide a newborn."

"This was only one courthouse. I'll try a neighboring county tomorrow. That'll be the last day government offices will be open before closing for Christmas. Mar, you decide which one."

She shrugged. "I don't know. Snohomish is to the north. Pierce is to the south." She waffled between the two. Neither stood out to her, so she shrugged again and held out her hands. "Snohomish?"

Ken gave an approving nod. "Snohomish it is. I have a feeling what we're searching for is out there somewhere, but I think it could be adoption information, not a birth or death certificate."

"I hope you're right." Mar definitely wanted to find something by Christmas or at least New Years.

Mindy tapped her finger on her lips. "I've been thinking. What if Dr. Thomas knew someone he wanted to give the baby to? Perhaps someone in his family who had just lost a baby or had a miscarriage. If that were the case, would he have filed it as a birth to cover up what he did?"

Ken raised his eyebrows. "He could have. I'll look for birth, death, and adoptions."

Mar's heart sank. "Mindy, that's so upsetting, I can hardly stand it. The worse thing is, it sounds so probable, it may be exactly what happened." How could people be so callous?

Depending on which card was drawn, it could have been Mar separated from her family. She shivered and sent up a quick prayer of thanks.

Chapter Five

Mar reveled in having friends so willing to jump in and help her at a moment's notice. Especially Ken who barely knew her and had spent most of the day at a musty courthouse fishing for information for her. No wonder her bestie was so enamored with this easygoing man. He almost didn't seem like a lawyer. He must really like Mindy to do all that for a relative stranger.

Mindy glanced at her watch. "It's past five-thirty. My mom and dad expect Mar and me for dinner in less than an hour. You, too, Ken, if you don't have other plans."

"I would love to meet your family. I'll call my sister so she knows not to expect me." Ken stepped to the wall phone and completed his call. "All set."

Mindy stood. "Great. Let's get our coats and go. Let us know your schedule for the rest of your vacation, Ken, so we can coordinate. I wouldn't want to upset your sister by monopolizing your time."

He grabbed Mindy's coat and held it for her. "It's not a problem. I'll spend Christmas day with them, but Jeanne and Robert are busy with the kids and some of his relatives who are local. It's probably best if I'm not in the way too much. I sprang this visit on them at the last minute."

"Sounds good." Mindy headed outside with Ken.

Mar doubted the pair would even notice if she didn't follow. She swung on her coat and locked up.

Mindy stopped at her Chevy. "Oops. I forgot I don't have the keys."

Ken opened the driver's door for her and handed over the keys.

"You can drive if you want, Ken."

"No, it's your car."

While the pair quibbled over who would take charge of the vehicle, Mar climbed in behind the driver's seat, leaving the front for the budding romance.

When Mindy finally slid in behind the wheel, he closed the door.

Before Mar could close hers, Ken stood like a statue with his hand on the top of the window frame as though unsure what to do. "I was going to sit back there."

Mar quickly fastened her seatbelt. "You're company, you should have the front."

Shrugging, he closed the door, then rounded the vehicle and settled himself in the passenger side.

In about two minutes, Mindy pulled into her folks' driveway.

As they got out of the car, Ken hesitated. "I hope your parents like me. I didn't bring anything for them."

"Not necessary." Mindy took his arm, tugging him toward the side entrance. "Don't worry. I've told them only nice things about you, and they'll be glad you came for dinner. Mom and Dad think it's great you help me so much at work and with my studies."

Mar hung back, waiting until the others reached the house, giving Mindy's folks a chance to focus on Ken.

In a chipper voice, Mindy introduced him to her parents.

Ken shook Tom's hand. "I'm pleased to meet you both, Mr. and Mrs. Stevens."

Tom clasped Ken's shoulder. "We aren't formal around here. Call us Tom and Susan."

Mar studied the young couple to gauge if her suspicions were correct. Everything about the pair said Ken was in love with Mindy, but she still saw him as nothing more than a dear friend.

Mar closed the gap and entered the house. "Thanks for inviting me for supper all the time. It's like I'm a real part of the family."

"Dear sweet Margaret." Susan pulled her in for a hug. "You are a very real part of this family. Haven't we welcomed you ever since you were six years old?"

Mindy's dad hooked his arm around Mar's shoulders and squeezed her from the side. "Yes. Sometimes I think of you girls as almost twins. Never met two people so much alike."

Strange he should use the word *twins* when he knew nothing of her search. Mar and Mindy did have birthdays three days apart and used to like to wear matching outfits.

Unaware of her musings, he continued. "I've thought of myself as your dad ever since George was killed in that airline crash when you and Mindy were ten. Your mother never seemed interested in remarrying, and we all enjoyed our friendship. We always felt both of you were an extension of our family."

"I feel the same way." They had been a huge comfort when Dad died and again when Mom did. "I hope you'll enjoy having Ken around for a good long time." Mar gave Mindy's parents another hug and shucked off her coat.

Tom and Susan exchanged a surprised glance but didn't probe. They would likely wait to ask questions until later when Ken had returned to his sister's. Tom gestured toward Ken. "Take off your coat, and make yourself at home. We've been looking forward to meeting the man who has taken such good care of our daughter."

Ken turned pink clear up to the roots of his sun-faded, white-blonde hair. "Thanks, I've been looking forward to meeting you also. I've wanted to tell you how smart and industrious your daughter is and how nice it is to be working with her. She won't have much trouble, if any, with the bar exam. You can be proud of her. We all are at the office."

Mindy chuckled. "Gee, Ken, for a minute I thought you were talking about my sister, Sandy, at least until you got to the part about the bar exam and the office." She glanced around. "Where is Sandy?"

"You know our little ray of sunshine." Tom gave an indulgent smile. "Sandy had to get in another day on the slopes before Santa comes. She went up to Crystal with some of her friends who are home for the holidays. If they stay for night skiing, she'll probably be home between ten-thirty and eleven. It may be threatening rain down here, but I'm sure it's beautiful up there."

"Regardless of when she's coming home, we're eating with or without her." Susan motioned everyone out of the back entry. "Dinner will be ready soon. Let's go into the living room and get acquainted."

The lovely room had a bright rag rug and early American-style furniture now accented with holly, fir boughs, and brass ornaments in honor of the season. Mindy and Mar sat at opposite ends of the couch, legs curled under, like mirror images. Tom and Susan each took a wing chair on either side of the fireplace with Ken choosing a hassock near Mindy's end of the couch.

Tom and Susan were soon engaged in conversation with Ken. He told them how he had graduated from Ohio State and earned his law degree from UCLA. He now worked for Stone and Perkins in Oakland, where he'd recently made junior partner, and now at thirty-three, he was doing well. "I've been able to help my parents with college for my younger brother and sister. This year I plan to give them a trip out to California for their fortieth anniversary. I have a great family, and we've all turned out okay."

If that wasn't a resume for the position of son-in-law, Mar didn't know what would be.

Susan rose. "Thank you, Ken, for telling us so much about you and your life. I'm sure you know quite a bit about us from Mindy, and you'll probably learn a lot more in the next few days. I think dinner's ready. Mindy and Margaret, will you girls help me carry in the food? Tom, you and Ken can set the table and meet us in the dining room."

In the kitchen, Susan pinned her daughter with a look. "Ken seems like a nice fellow, but it was almost as though he was interviewing for a job. He told us so much about himself."

Mindy merely shrugged.

"Maybe he thought of it that way." Mar smiled. "Don't you have any openings around here? Like for son-in-law or something?"

Susan's jaw hung loose, and Mindy swatted at Mar's shoulder. Just as Mindy opened her mouth, likely to scold Mar, the kitchen door opened.

Tom peered in. "Table's set. Anything else I can do to help?"

Susan handed him a bowl of vegetables and ushered everyone into the dining room.

Mindy, appearing somewhat shaken from Mar's comment, leaned toward her and whispered vehemently, "You just wait 'til I get you alone. You know Ken and I are *just* friends."

Mar whispered back in a sunny voice, "Sure, but remember *Que Sera Sera*." She scooted past her bestie before she could retaliate.

Susan pinched her lips. "What will be?"

Mindy pulled out her dining chair and shot Mar a warning glance. "Oh, you know," Mar answered as she sat. "Life, love, the future."

Susan clucked her tongue. "You girls and your secret codes."

Once settled, Tom said grace.

Mar enjoyed the baked salmon, vegetables, salad, rolls, and rice. Several times during the meal, Mindy glared. Mar responded with a cheeky smile.

Susan stood. "Who's ready for dessert? Cake and ice cream?"

Groans rippled around the table.

Susan chuckled. "Dessert can wait. If you four will clear the table, I'll start the coffee."

Once everything was taken care of, Susan loaded full cups on a tray.

Ken moved quickly to her side and picked up the flat shallow platter. "Let me get that for you."

"Why, thank you."

Everyone settled back in the same places they'd occupied before dinner as Ken circled the room, offering coffee to each person before retaking his seat on the hassock.

Mar wrapped her cold fingers around the warm mug. The young man had made points with Susan and likely Tom as well. One smart cookie.

A short time later, the front door swung open wide, and Sandy burst into the room. "I'm home!"

Like everyone else, Mar turned to see the lovely young girl—cheeks flushed from the cold, sparkling blue eyes, and light-brown hair with red highlights.

Sandy removed her ski jacket and draped it over her arm. "I suppose the evening is over." She zeroed in on the first-time guest and waved. "This must be Ken. I'm Sandy, Mindy's kid sister."

Had Mindy told everyone but Mar about Ken? Being left out stung, but then she wasn't a real member of this family, only an honorary one.

Susan stood. "Did you eat, sweetheart?"

Sandy nodded. "We grabbed burgers on our way back."

"Good. Then you are just in time for cake and ice cream."

Sandy cringed. "Sorry, Mom. I finished off the ice cream. I meant to replace it but forgot." She swung her coat back on. "I'll run to the store and get some. Ken, why don't you come with me so I can get to know you? I've been looking forward to meeting this brainy guy."

Mindy shook her head. "Sandy, I'm sure he doesn't want to go."

Ken rose slowly. "I don't mind. She can tell me stories about you."

Mindy jumped up. "I'll drive. Mar, why don't you come too?" She gave Mar a meaningful look.

Mar wasn't ready for Mindy's retaliation to her son-in-law comment. "It doesn't take four people to pick out ice cream. I'll stay here with your folks where my life isn't in danger."

With a puzzled expression, Ken turned to Mar. "Mindy's a good driver. I don't think your life will be in danger unless you're worried about the holiday traffic."

Susan gave Mar a sideways glance. "Ken, I don't think Mindy's driving has anything to do with what Mar means. It's a private joke between them."

Mar piped up. "I want to catch your folks up on my mystery."

Susan's and Tom's expressions both turned quizzical.

Mindy and Ken opened their mouths to speak, but Sandy tugged them toward the door. "Come on. The sooner we go, the sooner we'll have cake."

"Coats, Sandy. We need coats." Mindy heaved a sigh.

Ken held Mindy's while she slipped into it then swung his own on.

Mar caught Sandy's attention and pointed to Ken and mouthed, "He's a keeper."

Sandy inclined her head in understanding, then pointed to herself that she, too, would judge his worthiness.

Letting Sandy and Ken go first, Mindy glanced back at Mar with narrowed eyes but spoke in a sweet voice. "I'll see you when I return." The three left.

Mar turned to Tom and Susan. Time to catch them up on her conundrum. "I don't know if Mindy's had a chance to tell you what I uncovered about my mom."

They both shook their heads, but Tom spoke. "I am considerably intrigued."

Mar filled them in on all she had learned the past couple of days. "Did Mom ever mention to either of you about another baby?"

"Never." Susan's eyes widened.

Tom squinted slightly as though thinking. "I can't believe George or your mother never said anything about this. Are you sure?"

As sure as she could be. "That's why I'm searching, to uncover the truth. I can't stop thinking that I have a brother or sister somewhere who is even more in the dark than I am and doesn't even know it." Or perhaps, her twin was also searching for a missing piece of themself.

Susan inclined her head. "Don't get your hopes up too much. It would hurt my motherly heart to see you devastated. As you said, there isn't any real proof there was a second baby. For your sake, I do hope there was, and you find her or him."

Tom's expression held sympathy. "I can imagine how much all this is on your mind. It's a real head-scratcher."

Mar touched her chest. "You startled me when you equated Mindy and me to twins."

He huffed a breath that was almost a laugh. "Twins has a whole new meaning for me now."

Susan gave her husband a sideways glance before returning her attention to Mar. "We didn't know your mother then. We moved here just before you and Mindy started school. Even though we were close to your parents, especially your mother after your dad's death, nothing about another child was ever mentioned. This is an incredible mystery. Although it doesn't affect us personally, it matters to us because of how we love you. We want to help you in any way we can."

"Thank you so much for listening and understanding. Your support means a lot to me." Feeling the discussion was over, Mar moved to get up, but Susan stopped her. "You stay right here, young lady. I want clarification on your remark about an opening for a son-in-law." She lifted an eyebrow. "Spill the beans."

Cornered. No escape. "I've spent the last two days with them, and I feel comfortable around Ken. At first, I didn't notice anything between them, but I was suspicious of the way Mindy talked about him. Then, tonight when we were coming into the house, I hung back a little and watched them. Even though Mindy insists she and Ken are nothing more than friends, I'm sure Ken is head over heels in love with her. He's pretty good at covering it up, but when he thinks she's not paying attention, anyone can see it in his blue eyes. He's so proud and very protective of her. And why would he help me, a stranger, if not for his feelings for her? It's the only thing that makes sense."

Tom had a pensive expression. "You could be right. He did seem nervous and eager to make a favorable impression on us. I remember feeling much the same way when I met Susan's folks. Although, she already knew how I felt about her. Are you sure Mindy doesn't have a clue yet?"

Mar shook her head. "I asked her a couple of times. She denied it and glowered at me as though I'd told her to throw herself into a volcano."

"I, for one, hope she keeps on denying it." Tom leaned forward. "Her degree and passing the bar are the two most important things in her life right now. My guess is that she sees Ken as a means to those ends."

Susan heaved a sigh. "Well, that's not very romantic."

"I merely think it's best if she concentrates on her studies until she has her degree. She doesn't need distractions."

"True." Susan conceded. "But women are able to focus on more than one thing at a time. How do you think I took care of our three children, cleaned the house, and had supper on the table when you got home from work?"

"Because you are wonderful." Tom rose and gave his wife a kiss then retook his seat.

Mar had a few vague memories of tender moments such as these between her parents. She wished she had been paying better attention and had more of them. "I'll be careful what I say to her. I don't want to spoil anything going on between them or Mindy's degree. Besides, I have enough business of my own to keep me occupied."

Susan nodded. "I agree we should be careful what we say. We don't want to scare him off. He's been beneficial to both you and Mindy. We love you and are praying for you to find all the answers you need as soon as possible."

A little while later, car doors slammed and feet scampered in from the side door. Two laughing sisters tumbled into the room followed by a smiling Ken with a grocery bag.

Susan served up the cake with Sandy as her helper, adding a dollop of tin roof sundae ice cream or rocky road or chocolate chip mint. True to character, Sandy had gone overboard in replacing the ice cream she'd eaten.

After everyone had stuffed themselves with dessert, Ken stood. "I should get back to my sister's. May I use your phone?"

Tom and Susan glanced at each other and then at Mindy as though perplexed.

Ken answered their unspoken question. "I need to call a cab."

Mindy waved off that idea. "You can take my Blazer."

"I don't want to cut your visit with your parents and sister short."

Sandy yawned. "I'm tired, I've been up since four." And being Sandy, she hugged them all. When she wrapped her arms around Mar, she whispered in her ear. "I like Ken a lot. Let's figure out a way to keep him in the family." She headed for bed.

Mindy must have heard because she opened her mouth, facing Mar, but before she could get the words out, Mar whispered. "Sorry, Mindy. I got carried away with myself. I feel as though I've known Ken for ages and thought it would be great if he were hanging around for years to come. It's up to you though, so I apologize."

Mindy stood there for a moment with a stunned expression. "Thanks." She turned to her parents. "I'm going stay at Mar's again if that's all right."

"That's fine." Susan waved her consent. "We'll still see you Christmas Eve, as usual, won't we? You, too, Ken."

Ken gave a nod. "I'll see what my sister has planned, but I'm sure it will be fine."

Mar put on her coat. "We should go so Ken can get on the road. Thanks for supper."

Mindy and Ken followed her.

At her house, Mar bid Ken good night.

He looked her straight in the eyes. "We're going to figure this out. The answers are out there."

Mindy nodded. "And so is your twin."

"Thanks. I appreciate all you both are doing for me." Mar made eye contact with Ken. "Sorry I'm taking you away from your vacation plans, and that you aren't going to learn to ski this trip."

He shrugged. "I can learn to ski another time."

Mar left Mindy and Ken to say their own goodbyes.

Later, Mar's mind whirled with possibilities as she lay in bed. Did she have a twin or not? Was he or she still alive? Did she have a brother or sister? Which did she want? Mindy was already like a sister, so perhaps a brother. But a sister would be nice. Would she have similar interests? So many possibilities.

Chapter Six

Even with her eyes still closed the next morning, Mar could tell it was light outside. She willed herself back to unconsciousness. The events and information from the past three days had tumbled around in her head 'til well after four a.m. No use. The headache from not sleeping refused to allow her any more rest.

When she pried her unwilling eyes open, the bed across the room sat neatly made but empty and the smell of coffee hung in the air. Mindy was up. Had Ken arrived early again?

What time is it? She blinked to get her eyes to focus on the red numbers.

10:17!

How had she slept in so long? Being awake most of the night, that was how. Heaving a sigh, she threw back the covers. Deciding to shower later, she dressed and headed for the coffee.

Mindy sat alone at the kitchen table.

"Morning." Mar glanced around. "I need coffee." That would help her throbbing head.

Mindy lowered the paper. "I'm not surprised. You tossed half the night. All you've learned recently must be . . . must be . . . I can't even imagine what it must be like. Chaos, for sure."

Mar poured herself a cup and took a deep, deep breath of the aroma. "Looks like Ken was here." The table was set for two. A grapefruit half at one place and the shell of the other half near Mindy. As well as what appeared to be home-baked muffins.

"Perhaps. But I don't know for sure. It could have been a Christmas elf who stopped by a couple of days early. There's a quiche in the warmer."

"Where's Ken?" Mar sat, sipping her coffee.

Mindy shrugged. "When I got up, the table was set, the coffee was brewed, and quiche was in the warmer." She picked up a slip of paper. "Says 'Sorry I missed you. Coffee's made and a Florentine quiche waits in the oven on warm. Have a great day. K.' Now I think 'K' stands for Kringle, therefore an elf."

"I'll buy that." Ken certainly was helpful like one.

"Come see." Mindy folded the newspaper to reveal the classifieds. "Our ad is in this morning's edition. I hope someone who knows the Swansons reads it and calls soon, I can hardly wait."

Her friend could hardly wait? Mar was giddy with anticipation. She carried her coffee to the table and buttered a blueberry muffin. Ken certainly was trying to sell himself to Mindy. "You realize Ken's a great cook and handy to have around."

Mindy rolled her eyes. "Of course. I've known him longer than you, and I'm the one who brought him home for the holidays."

Was that a hint of possessiveness in her friend's voice? How she couldn't see what was so clear to everyone else was beyond Mar's comprehension.

Mindy rattled the paper. "Just look at the ad."

Mar peered over Mindy's shoulder to see the personal column and zeroed in on the circled spot. *Please let the right people see this.*

She took a bite of her muffin and a few crumbs rained down on Mindy's shoulder and arm.

Her friend swiped at the debris. "Hey, watch it. Either sit down and eat breakfast or put that muffin down."

"Sorry." Mar set the tasty delight on the plate set out for her and brushed the crumbs from her hands. She leaned closer to the ad. "It looks right. I can't wait to hear from somebody. Anybody."

"Even that nice man at the paper who took extra care gathering your information for this?"

"He did no such thing. He was only doing his job." Mar sat, wishing Mindy would drop that. She neither expected nor wanted him to call her. Time to turn the tables. "So, do you really think of Ken as only a friend?"

Mindy offered a disdainful look. "I don't understand why you keep making remarks about Ken. I know he's great. After all, he's my best friend in the world next to you, and I've been stuck with you forever."

"So, I guess you think if I'm your best friend forever, he's in for the long haul too? Don't you suppose he might someday want to do more than help you study and cook for you? Like get married and have a couple of kids or something?"

"Shut up and eat your breakfast, Mar. Ken and I don't feel that way. We just like each other better than anyone else."

For being so smart, Mindy could be a real dunce sometimes. "You may not think so Mindy, but Ken is certainly in love with you." *Oops.* She wasn't supposed to say anything about that, but she couldn't help herself. This twin stuff had her rattled. In for a penny, in for a pound. "I see how he looks at you when he thinks no one else is watching. Why else would he come early to cook and go to the courthouse for me, if it wasn't to please you?" Ken wouldn't wait around forever with no encouragement.

She knew how single-minded her friend could be even to the point of missing out on something else and regretting it. Since she had begun, she might as well stay the course. "He's given up his skiing holiday to help us find the answer to my problem. If he merely wanted to learn to ski, he could have hired an instructor or gone to ski classes, as we did back in junior high. I'm sure he chose to help us so he can be with you. If someone doesn't realize he's a keeper, she might lose him someday."

Mindy huffed an exaggerated, long breath. "I told you we like to be with each other because we enjoy doing things together, and that's why he's decided to wait until we have time to go skiing with him."

"Okay, Mindy." Mar turned in her chair and took hold of both of her friend's hands. "I'll put it this way, think of how you'd feel if you knew Ken would never be part of your life again. Don't answer now, but try to realize how it would be for you if Ken falls in love with someone else, gets married, and never pals around with you anymore. Think about it."

Mindy frowned and pulled her hands free. "I don't want to do this now, Mar! You know I can't think of anything else but finishing school and passing the bar exam. I decided long ago to put my whole life on hold until I'd accomplished what I'd set out to do. Why are you trying to make it harder for me than it already is? Ken is always there to help me through the rough spots, back me up, and boost my morale!"

"Counselor, I rest my case." Mar crossed to the stove to dish up some of the quiche Ken had kindly made for them. Returning to the table, she ate in silence.

Mindy sat for a long time, not saying a word, seeming to focus on the hills of west Seattle but likely searching her own heart.

Once finished, Mar cleaned her plate and put it in the dishwasher. Then she sat next to Mindy and touched her hand. "I'm not trying to hurt you or make you feel bad. I just don't want you to miss one of the best things that may ever happen to you. I remember what you said about putting your life on hold, but here you are at a place where you can see the finish line ahead. I feel like it's time for you to at least begin to examine the future possibilities. What have you been sitting here musing over for so long?"

"I wasn't ready to hear what you had to say about the future, but I realize we're almost thirty years old now, and I'm going to have that law degree in the not-too-distant future. So, you're right. It's about time for me to stop thinking my life will always be the same. Stop thinking the future will never come."

"What does that mean? Have you made any decisions or realizations yet?"

"Well, you're absolutely right about my not wanting to have a life without Ken. So, if he really feels what you say he does about me, I guess it's time I figure out how *I* feel about *him*."

A slow smile broke across Mar's face, and she got up to give Mindy a hug. "I already know. And you'll puzzle it all out and come to the right conclusion for yourself. I pushed you so hard because I love you, and I think Ken is the best."

"You know, Mar, I already realized Ken is the greatest guy I've ever known, but I hadn't thought ahead to graduation and how our lives will change. What if he doesn't want to move up here?"

"Ken would follow you to the ends of the earth, dear Mindy."

Her friend pressed her lips together. "You have far more confidence in this than I do, but we need to table this for more pressing matters. We told Mom we would bring dessert for Christmas Eve. We could make or buy one."

"Why don't you make that fruit flan and pick up some ice cream too?" Then they both burst out laughing, and Mar said, "I think Sandy has the ice cream front covered."

"If she hasn't eaten it all by then."

Mar gazed at Mindy with wide eyes and another round of laughter ensued.

Once they controlled themselves, the two bustled around, gathering the tools they needed for the flan and checking ingredients. Then Mar said, "Let's make it on a sponge cake and roll it like a jelly roll."

"Great idea. Do we have everything?"

Mar made a quick list. "If you'll start the cake part, I'll run to the store for the strawberries."

Mindy saluted. "Aye, aye, captain."

After returning, Mar cut up and steamed the fresh fruit, while Mindy poured the batter on a long sheet pan and popped it into the oven.

Much later, the fruit and custard-filled roll was safely in the refrigerator.

Mindy glanced at the kitchen clock. "Wow, that was no short-term project. It'll be dark soon. I wonder where Ken is? I wish he'd call so I know he's safe."

Mar patted Mindy's arm. "I'm sure he's fine. He probably stopped off at his sister's or something. Do you want to help me go through the names we got at the funeral home?"

Two hours later, the kitchen door opened, and Ken came in, a downcast expression on his usually cheerful face. Both women turned to him expectantly.

He shook his head. "I couldn't find anything today. I didn't even run across any possibilities in Snohomish County. We'll have to reorganize and search somewhere else after everyone's back from Christmas but before they're off for New Year."

Mar's shoulders drooped. "I feel like we're up against a brick wall."

Ken sighed. "I know that's how it seems, but remember, it's still the holiday season. Let's not get too discouraged for a while yet." He held up a large paper sack in one hand. "I did bring supper. Chinese. I know what Mindy likes but had to guess for you, Mar."

"Mar doesn't like Chinese food." Mindy stared at him and whispered under her breath to Mar. "You were right—about everything."

Mar mouthed. "It's okay."

"I'm such a terrible person." With unshed tears, Mindy stood and hurried from the room.

Ken didn't move. His eyes were as large as saucers. "Was she crying?"

So, he'd noticed the tears brimming in Mindy's eyes.

"What did I do wrong?"

"Nothing. She's fine. I had a little distressing news for her earlier. She just needs a minute or two to collect herself."

After a moment of awkward silence, Ken said, "I'm sorry I didn't know you don't like Chinese food."

Mar waved her hand through the air. "Don't worry about it. I'll heat up the left-over pizza from the other night."

"Are you sure? I feel awful."

Probably more because Mindy was upset than the food choice.

Mar put two slices of pizza on a plate and popped it into the microwave. "Nuked pizza has sort of a rubbery texture and is chewy. I'm weird. I like it that way."

Mindy returned with the appearance that nothing was amiss a few minutes earlier.

The microwave beeped.

Mar rescued her dinner. "I'm going to take this to my room." She slipped away to her bedroom to give Mindy and Ken a chance to talk. Excitement coursed through her at the pair in her kitchen acknowledging their feelings for each other. She prayed her friends sorted things out between them, and she also prayed that answers to her puzzle would come tomorrow. And an important phone call.

Chapter Seven

Mar's eyes popped open to a dark room. When had she fallen asleep? The last thing she recalled was reading one of her dad's letters while enjoying chewy, leftover pizza. Mindy must have turned off the light. The red glow of the clock illuminated her plate with half of a slice left. The numbers read 5:57. It was morning already? This was the first full night's sleep she'd gotten since this whole mystery began.

For the second morning in a row, the bed across the room sat empty and neatly made if she had interpreted the shadows correctly. Mindy had never been an early riser. Her friend joked that she would be a morning person *if* morning began at noon. So where was she?

Still in her clothes from yesterday, Mar threw back the blanket that Mindy had likely draped over her, made a quick trip to the bathroom, and padded out to the kitchen then the living room.

Mindy lay curled on the couch covered with an afghan. Why was she sleeping out here?

Mar would ask her later. No sense poking the bear unnecessarily. She returned to the kitchen. A cup of hot chocolate sounded divine.

Two hours later, as Mar finished reading the newspaper, Mindy shuffled into the kitchen, wearing the sweater and slacks from the day before. "Where's Ken?"

"I assume at his sister's." Mar folded the paper and set it aside. "It appears we both slept in our clothes. Why did you crash on the couch?"

Mindy yawned. "I was snuggling with Ken, talking about the future. I must have drifted off. He evidently put the afghan on me before he left. How sweet of him."

He did get points for that. That boy was racking up the good deeds.

"Can I assume it was you who covered me?"

"I went in to check on you. You were asleep, and I didn't want you to get cold. Ken and I were making plans to go out today as our first official date. You were right. He does really like me. And I couldn't be more thrilled."

"I'm so happy for you. But don't let your grades slip, or I'll have to answer to your parents for telling you about Ken's feelings."

"They know?"

Mar nodded.

"I don't have far to go. I can stay focused until the end. Ken will make sure of it."

"Have you guys decided what you're going to do today?"

Mindy had the expression of a smitten schoolgirl. "We're going out to the science center first, so we'll lie on the floor, watching the laser show. After that, we'll eat at the food circus, ride the monorail, and go to a movie, then, have dessert somewhere quiet."

"Sounds like a big day. I don't think you'll have time for all that. Remember we have Christmas Eve dinner with your parents."

"It doesn't matter what we do. We could sit on a park bench the entire day, and I would be happy."

Mar had no doubt about that. "You better go shower and dress so you're ready when Ken arrives."

With a huge grin, Mindy scurried down the hall.

An hour and a half later, Mar waved the couple goodbye.

Mindy halted at the door. "I feel bad for abandoning you. Maybe we shouldn't go."

"Nonsense. Go." Mar motioned them toward the door.

"But what about finding your twin?"

Ken remained silent, apparently not wanting to get between friends.

That left it up to Mar. "It's Christmas Eve. Even I know we can't make much progress today. Go. Have fun."

"But you'll be all alone. Come with us."

Mar was *not* about to intrude on their first real date. "No. I'll be fine. I'm going to sort through Mom's room to gather a box of clothes for the women's shelter." Which had put her right back where this puzzle had started on Sunday.

"If you're sure." Mindy was being ridiculous.

Mar pressed her hands to Mindy's back. "Go. Before I decide to change the locks while you're gone."

Mindy opened her mouth, but before her friend could say anything, Mar stopped her. "Not one more word, young lady. Don't come home until you've had fun." Mar gave Ken an imploring look.

He turned to Mindy. "We've been given an order."

"And you'll be back in time to go to your house for the Christmas Eve festivities," Mar added.

With a huge sigh, Mindy finally quit resisting and left.

Alone at last.

With a fresh cup of hot chocolate in hand, Mar stepped into Mom's bedroom. Over the last few days, she had gotten to know her parents like she never had while either of them was alive.

On the floor sat three boxes. Each labeled as to its contents' fate—*giveaway*, *keep*, and *toss*. The *keep* container sat empty. *Toss* had a scattering of trash within. The *giveaway* one had been half full before Mar had come across the documents, letters, and diaries. She set her chocolate on the dresser and retrieved a few items she didn't want to part with now.

Before, she had pictured herself giving most of it away. Now, she wanted to hold on to little treasures of her mother. Part of her longed to keep everything. She wouldn't, but she wanted to. Instead of being ruthless as she sorted through the clothes hanging in the closet, she ached with each article she placed lovingly in the *giveaway* box. She kept reminding herself that these would help the women in crisis at the shelter far more than herself.

After the hangers were emptied, she reached up to the shelf and pulled down the suitcase, extra blankets, a pile of *National Geographic*, and a scattering of smaller boxes. The suitcase would hold the clothes Mar had decided to keep for now. She kept an afghan and quilt made by her grandma and put the other blankets with the clothes for the shelter. The magazines went with the *toss* items. The rest of the shelf consisted of mostly odds and ends, until she got to a shoebox which had been in the far corner, under a ratty blanket. Almost as though it were being hidden.

Wondering what kind of shoes they could be, Mar removed the lid and stared at the contents. From front to back, what appeared to be letters and cards sat upright. More of her parents' correspondence?

Since her mom's bed was cluttered with the morning's work, Mar took the container to her own room to spread out on the bed. She thumbed through the neatly filed envelopes. Not one had a name nor address—completely blank. Hidden behind the last was a pair of white baby booties and a small white rattle. Neither appeared to have been used much if at all. Were these some of Mar's things as a baby?

She plucked the first envelope—yellowed with age. She slipped the single sheet of paper out and unfolded it. Dated one month after Mar's birth.

Dear Little One...

Strange she hadn't used Mar's name.

I have thought of you every day since your birth. I did not want you to think you were forgotten simply because you aren't with me.

Mar sucked in a breath. This was written to her twin.

I ache that I never got to hold you. But I keep you in my heart and see your face reflected in your sister's.

Mom continued to pour out her heart to the child she'd lost.

The subsequent envelopes held birthday cards that started the same—*Happy Birthday, Little One*. Then they went on to let Mar's twin know he or she wasn't forgotten, and Mom pictured what the child would be doing if he or she had lived.

Mar wiped away tears. "Oh, Mom, I'm so sorry for not realizing you were in such pain over the loss of your baby. But the good news is, your other child may still be alive. I'm going to find him or her. At the very least, discover what happened." Just because her twin hadn't died at birth, didn't mean something bad hadn't happened since then.

Once the letters and cards had been read and neatly tucked back inside the shoebox, Mar set it on the end of her bed and returned to Mom's room. She needed to get these donations delivered before she changed her mind and kept it all. The collection filled the backseat of her car. As she left the house for the last time, she grabbed a slice of the quiche and ate it cold from her hand. Surprisingly, it still tasted great.

On her way back from dropping off the items at the shelter, she passed a little curio antique shop she'd driven by almost daily but had never been in. It piqued her interest. She'd done a good day's work and decided to treat herself with a little look. She drove around the block and parked nearby.

In the window sat an elaborately designed picture frame made of pewter. It held a small garden scene drawn exquisitely in pastels. A young child sat in a swing, smiling. Mar stared at it and couldn't help but think of Mrs. Thomas. It would be perfect for her, and Mar could deliver it tomorrow. She went inside and purchased it.

Once back at home, the light on her answering machine blinked to indicate a message. She listened. A woman named Joan Taylor said Rose Swanson had been her daughter's teacher. Mar called the number but didn't get much more information. However, it was encouraging that someone had seen the ad and responded.

A little while later, Mindy and Ken arrived with wide smiles.

Mar was happy they'd had a good time. "So, how was your day? Were you able to go everywhere and do everything you had hoped to?"

"It was wonderful." Mindy's wistful expression warmed Mar's heart. "You were right. We didn't have time for everything, so we skipped the movie, but the laser show was great. I nearly went broke, trying food from all the different vendors at the food circus." Mindy grasped Mar's arm. "Oh, Mar, you should have seen the view from the monorail. And the fabulous dessert we had was *crème brûlée crepes*. Did you know they made those?" Mindy cringed. "Here I am going on and on. How was your day?"

Shrugging, Mar tried to sound nonchalant with a noncommittal noise, but she couldn't hold her excitement in any longer. "It was fantastic, aside from a few tears while I went through Mom's stuff. I viewed each thing differently than a few days ago." Her words tumbled almost one on top of the other in her enthusiasm to get it all out. "I took a box to the women's shelter, and on the way home, I picked up a gift for Mrs. Thomas that I plan to give her tomorrow."

Running out of air, Mar took a deep breath and continued. "But before that, I found an old shoebox in the top back part of the closet. Inside was a pair of white baby booties, a plastic rattle, and a whole stack of letters and cards, each in its own envelope. At first, I thought they were about me, but they weren't. They were for my twin. Mom wrote a letter every year on our birthday. They're beautiful." Mom had ached for the child she lost.

"Cards for your twin? That's wonderful." Mindy crinkled her eyebrows. "You got a gift for Mrs. Thomas?"

Mar took it from the bag and unwrapped the frame from the tissue. "What do you think?" She held it out for examination. "It's small enough to set on her night table or dresser. Will she like it?"

Mindy bent to study the picture more closely. "She'll love it."

Ken touched the frame, almost reverently. "I think it would be perfect for nearly anyone. Mrs. Thomas must be pretty special to you."

Instantly sobered, Mar glanced at Mindy, then at her new friend. "Not really. This is a bribe of sorts. Is it a bad idea? I thought perhaps she would be more willing to open up."

Ken shrugged. "Sometimes perseverance is the only way. Your motive might not be pure, but it is kind, and it may eventually pay off."

"After finding the birthday cards, I wanted to talk to her again. I'm hoping she'll have remembered something. You know, getting the old cognitive juices flowing." Mar turned to Mindy. "You'll come with me, won't you?"

"Of course. You've had quite a day."

"Oh, but there's more. Joan Taylor, who knew the Swansons several years ago, replied to our ad and left a message."

Ken raised his eyebrows. "That was fast."

"I know. I called her back. She said Rose Swanson had been her daughter's teacher, up on the Okanogan at Omak. She doesn't know if Rose is still working there, but it's a place to start looking."

"That's progress."

Mar's enthusiasm soared. "I sure hope either the Swansons or someone else who knew them responds to the ad. This wondering is driving me crazy. I suspect the Swansons won't have any answers about my twin though, because if my mom didn't know where the other baby went, neither would they."

"This is great." Mindy pulled a face. "I hate to break up this party, but my folks are expecting us for dinner."

Mar extended her index finger. "Also, don't tell your parents about you and Ken yet."

Mindy pushed away the thought with her hands. "I won't."

Ken scrunched his eyes a bit. "Why not?"

"They won't like me having a distraction. They'll think I won't finish my degree."

Ken pressed his lips together. "I don't feel right lying to them."

"Not lying. We merely aren't going to tell them."

"Lying by omission?"

Mindy shook her head. "We just won't enter it into evidence yet. And no holding hands or anything like that. We act as though nothing has changed between us."

Ken thinned his lips. "If they ask, I won't perjure myself."

"I wouldn't expect you to." Mindy raised up and gave him a peck on the cheek. "But they won't. You'll be safe."

Grabbing the fruit roll dessert they'd made yesterday, Mar retrieved her keys from her purse. "Since Mindy and I will be staying at her house, I'll take my car over too. That way when you leave, Ken, we'll still have transportation."

After the quick trip and hustling inside the house, Mar nudged Mindy and whispered, "I just had a terrible thought."

Mindy unzipped her coat. "What?"

"Your mom's not going to serve *Lutefisk* for Christmas Eve dinner and tell Ken it's a tradition, is she?" She mentally grimaced at the thought of the Scandinavian lye-soaked, boiled cod that became a gelatinous consistency.

Mindy's eyes widened to the size of walnuts, and she sidled up to her mother. "Mom, tell me we aren't having *Lutefisk* for dinner."

Susan thinned her lips. "Of *course* not, *I* wouldn't do that to the poor unsuspecting man. He seems like a nice fellow."

The evening went without incident. If either Tom or Susan suspected any new developments between Mindy and Ken, they didn't act as such.

Mar spent most of the evening distracted by recollections of the letters written to her twin. Many of the statements in them were things Mom had said to Mar over the years. She felt closer to her twin already even though they hadn't met.

Yet.

Chapter Eight

After ransacking stockings the following morning and gobbling down waffles with strawberries and a mountain of whip cream, Mar and Mindy dressed for their trip to see Mrs. Thomas. Mar swung on her coat and headed out the door with her friend on her heels. "I hope she remembers me from the other day."

Before long, Mar pulled into the nursing home parking lot. Mindy walked beside her into the festively decorated reception area before noon. Some of the residents sat with family members, opening gifts or visiting. Mrs. Thomas wasn't among them.

Mar crossed to the nurse's station and learned that the old lady had refused to join the others on this jolly occasion because she had no friends or family to spend the day with. How sad to not have anyone on Christmas. Mar was doubly glad she chose today to visit this lonely soul and nurture the serendipitous opportunity to be alone with her to discover what she knew. Finding Mrs. Thomas's room, Mar's heart ached for the hunched form slouched in a chair.

With a bolstering deep breath, Mar strode in and spoke in a bright voice. "Merry Christmas." She held out the small package with the picture in the nice frame for the woman's bedside table.

Mrs. Thomas pulled her arms tight to her chest. "Who are you? What do you want?"

Mar crouched in front of her. "We came to wish you Merry Christmas and to give you this." She set the package on the granny-square afghan on the woman's lap. "I'm Margaret Ross. I was here the other day."

The elderly woman's expression changed. "I know you, don't I?" Good. She remembered. Her gaze flickered to Mindy who stood a few feet away.

Mar nodded. "This is my friend, Mindy."

Mindy waved. "Hi. Merry Christmas."

Mrs. Thomas smiled. "It's nice to have visitors." She squinted at Mar. "I know your mother."

"That's right." Mar wasn't sure how much time she would have while the woman was coherent, so she jumped right in with her question. "When I visited the other day, I asked you about the time of my birth. I was hoping you might have remembered more you could tell me. Anything."

The gray-haired woman turned a wistful gaze toward the window, staring into the distance as though recalling the past. Her mouth curved in a slight smile, but the look in her eyes hinted at distress. As minutes ticked by, Mrs. Thomas sat quietly with that faraway expression.

What should Mar do? Unsure if she should prod her more, she took the frail hand of the white-haired lady. "Would you like to open your gift?"

Mrs. Thomas seemed to return and nodded.

Mar removed the ribbon and tape from the small package, then placed it back on her lap.

With wrinkled hands, she finished unwrapping the gift. Holding it up near her face, she first smiled as she slowly rubbed the smooth metal of the frame, then tears trickled down the wrinkles in her cheeks.

Taking a tissue from a box on the nightstand, Mar carefully patted them away. "Are you crying because you're sad? Have we done something to upset you, Mrs. Thomas?"

Shaking her head, Mrs. Thomas whispered in a small voice, "I'm happy, dear. No one has given me a present in a long time. This was sweet of you. It's so nice of you girls to visit me on Christmas."

Mar needed to bring this conversation back on track. "You said you knew my mother, Beth Johnson. You helped deliver me nearly thirty years ago. Do you remember?"

"Of course, dear." Mrs. Thomas patted Mar's cheek. "You are both lovely young ladies, but of course, you were such beautiful babies."

Both? Holding her breath, Mar couldn't believe what she had just heard. She stared directly into the wrinkled face. "There *were* two babies? Both girls? That's what you just said, right?" Mar wanted to make sure she wasn't talking about Mindy. Mar could hardly believe it. She had a sister.

Mrs. Thomas recoiled, and fear marred her previously calm expression. "I-I don't remember. I must have made a mistake."

"What's going on here?" a male voice barked from behind them.

Mar spun as she stood.

A tall, slender man with narrowed eyes and thinned lips had apparently entered silently. "What's wrong, Mrs. Thomas? Are these women bothering you?" Before Mrs. Thomas could say anything, he turned to Mar. "You must be the individual my nurse told me about. She said you were at the office, making accusations concerning Dr. and Mrs. Thomas. If you don't stop bothering her, I'll call the authorities and file a restraining order on her behalf."

Mar had made no accusations.

The man could be good looking if he chanced a smile, but in his present state, that was unlikely.

He addressed Mrs. Thomas again and, talking to her in a calming tone, assured her she wouldn't have any further problems with these people. He turned his glaring expression on Mar. "I'm Dr. Kevin Drake, Mrs. Thomas's physician. I came to check on her well-being and found you here harassing her. Leave now, or I'll be forced to take action." Not giving them any chance to explain, he ushered them from the room and shut the door.

Mar didn't know if she should be upset at being thrown out or ecstatic at learning she had a sister. After leaving the building, she got into her car, exited the parking lot, and pulled out into traffic without a word. When her brain finally scrambled together a thought, she glanced at her friend. "Well, if that doesn't beat it all. I suppose now I'll never find out the whole truth. He'll probably have me banned from the nursing home, and I sure won't find out anything from him or his nurse."

"Yeah. He was kind of upset, wasn't he? He was way overprotective of Mrs. Thomas. He didn't even ask us why we were there. Just assumed we were doing something wrong. Maybe if we give it a little time, he'll calm down, and you can explain it to him."

"Oh sure." Mar couldn't keep the sarcasm from her voice. "More likely he'll never let me near enough for that in this century!" Her spirits fell, and she wanted to cry.

"The upside is the next century is only a little over a year away."

Mar rolled her eyes. "Ha, ha."

"Sorry." Mindy cringed. "Even if we did have a run-in with that egotistical Dr. Drake, we learned your mother wasn't imagining things. You were beautiful *babies* is what she said, so both lived."

"You're probably right. We do know more than we did yesterday." Mar let out a deep sigh. "Because this means so much to me, any stumbling block seems like the Great Wall of China. I went nearly thirty years without knowing anything about having a sister, so I guess it won't kill me to go a little slower. I just want all the answers instantly."

"I know. It's still Christmas Day, so let's go help my mom with dinner. Johnny and his family will probably be at the house by now. My brother's kids will want to open the presents we have for them." Mindy gave Mar a sympathetic look. "Do you think you can forget about this experience and be happy the rest of the day?"

Mar pushed down the overwhelming chaos of emotions and rustled up a smile. "I promise to be cheery and not spoil the day."

"Thanks. I haven't seen any of them since August. I hope the kids missed me. They're growing so fast, it's hard to buy gifts when I'm not around them much anymore."

"I know." Mar turned onto Mindy's street. "Even though I see them fairly often, I'm always surprised at how fast they change. I see Johnny's wife, Cindy, more than any of them. She models for several of my accounts, and we have lunch sometimes when we're working at the same location. She's such a great person and gets more beautiful every time I see her."

"She always has been gorgeous." Mindy nodded. "I remember how envious I used to be when my brother was dating her back in high school, and I was the tagalong little sister eager for attention. I wanted to be just like her. No. I wanted to *be* her. Except for the dating my brother part."

"We all did." Mar pulled the car to a stop in front of the house.

Mindy unbuckled her seatbelt. "But now, I'm satisfied with who I am and happy to be about to earn my degree. I feel sometimes as though my life is only going to begin when I walk off that dais with my diploma in hand." She shook her head. "Wow, Mar, did I say my life's been on hold for almost thirty years? I think that makes me Sleeping Beauty or Rip Van Winkle."

"Definitely Sleeping Beauty. You would look terrible in a beard." Mar stifled a chuckle until Mindy laughed. No wonder Mindy'd had a hard time seeing Ken as anything more than a friend. At least not until post-graduation.

Mindy's life might have been on hold until she earned her degree, but Mar's had stopped when Mom died, and she hadn't even known it. She felt so alone. Searching for her sister was the kick-start she needed to get her life going again.

After hopping out of the car, Mar followed her best friend into the house. Mindy hoisted four-year-old Susie, while Mar picked up John Jr.

Little Susie, a blonde, blue-eyed imp, clapped her hands and gave Mindy a big hug. "Aunt Mindy, can we open our presents now? Grandma and Grandpa said we had to wait for you."

John Jr. blinked his baby blues at Mar. "Auntie Mar, presents now, pease!"

Mar hugged the toddler tightly. "Okay, honey, run and get Grandma and Grandpa, Mommy and Daddy, and Aunt Sandy. Tell them all, 'presents now.'"

The two little ones ran off, and in a few moments, everyone was gathered around the huge tree in the living room. Susie sat cross-legged on the floor as close as she could get to the gifts. With a careful eye on his big sister, John Jr. copied her.

Tom took his place next to the tree with his Santa hat on, ready to hand out presents. He reached under the festively decorated branches and distributed a package to each of the adults, then he turned to the squirming little ones. "I'll bet you think Santa has forgotten you, but I'm sure he must have left something for Susie and JJ." After pawing under the tree, he turned to the children. "No more presents."

Susie and JJ lay on the floor to see all the way under the tree and sat back up with pouts.

Mar and Mindy were in on Tom's little charade, and their gifts for the children had been tucked away for later.

He thumped his palm on his forehead. "How could I have forgotten Santa left something for the two of you in the garage?"

The two children jumped to their feet and ran as fast as possible through the kitchen and into the garage. By the time everyone arrived, they were staring in awe, with their blue eyes sparkling and little hands clasped in front of them at a real—though smaller than full-size—merry-go-round, complete with six animals. They included a smiling elephant, a yellow duck, a ferocious tiger, a green dragon, a spindly giraffe, and a roly-poly bear.

"Oh, Grandpa," Susie whispered. "Is it really ours? Did Santa really leave it for JJ and me?"

"Yes, Susie, he *really* did. He told me the elves made it, especially for the two of you." Tom's grandpa-smile almost reached from ear to ear. "Let's try it out. You two get the first ride! Hurry up, choose your animal, and hop on." As the children ran over to the carousel, he walked across the garage and plugged in the power. Susie chose the elephant, and JJ climbed up the yellow duck. Grandpa pulled a lever, and the carousel turned to the tune of "My Beautiful Balloon."

Mindy walked up close to her dad. "I'll bet they were the same elves that made that wonderful treehouse for Johnny, Sandy, and me, with the sandbox and spiral slide."

Tom's eyes twinkled at his daughter. "I'm pretty sure those were the ones."

"This must have taken you forever. When did you start?"

"I began planning it nearly two years ago and started some of the building and woodworking New Year's Day."

The lovely toy came slowly to a halt, and Tom called to the others. "There's a seat for everyone, so no fighting over the animals."

"I get the bear," Sandy called as she scrambled toward the carousel.

Mar and Mindy joined Sandy and the two small children, while Tom ran the controls. The others returned inside the house. Though it was a cold day, they had a great time riding, singing, and trading seats. Finally, as darkness settled in, and the lights of Seattle sparkled through the garage windows, Mar and Mindy each picked up one of the two tired children and went into the warm, welcoming house for Christmas dinner.

After everyone had eaten their fill and the children had opened their other presents, the little ones fell asleep in their parents' arms and were soon on their way home to their own beds. Mar and Mindy restored the dining room to its earlier holiday aura, put away all the leftovers that hadn't been sent home with John and Cindy, then came back to the living room where Tom and Susan relaxed with their usual cups of coffee. Susan sat at the piano, situated in the bay window alcove, and played a quiet serenade. Tom perched on the bench next to her with an adoring expression on his face.

Stopping just inside the door, Mindy whispered, "It seems we aren't needed here anymore." She pointed the way they had come.

Mar caught Tom and Susan's attention. "We are going to head over to my house."

Susan waved. "Thanks for all your help."

Tom nodded. "Merry Christmas."

Once in the hall, they grabbed their things and returned to Mar's house.

Back at her own home, Mar shucked her coat. "What a day. From the top to the bottom and back up again on an emotional roller coaster!" When the encounter with the obnoxious Dr. Drake flashed through her mind, a fit of laughter overtook her.

Mindy stared at her as though she had lost her mind.

Mar couldn't help herself. His expression had been so stern. Way more fuss than was called for. She tamped down the giggles so she could speak. "You know, even with all that self-righteousness, Dr. Kevin Drake was kind of cute with that swoop of dark hair falling over his forehead. I'll probably never get a chance to explain it all to him, so I guess it doesn't matter."

"You know," Mindy bit her bottom lip, "I thought he was a fox too. I was afraid to say anything because you were so upset. I didn't want to make you madder."

"I wasn't mad, just hurt that someone would think I was being mean or cruel to a senior citizen. And when he got so indignant, I didn't know how to deal with it. Then the next thing I knew, he pushed us out into the hall and shut the door. At that point, there wasn't more we could do."

Later, as Mar allowed herself to drift toward sleep, Mrs. Thomas's words swirled in her head. *You are both lovely young ladies, but of course, you were such beautiful babies.*

You are *both lovely young ladies.*

That must mean Mrs. Thomas knows Mar's twin as an adult. Had she kept in contact with her? Did she live around here?

What an exciting thought.

Chapter Nine

The next morning, Ken had arrived and cooked them a breakfast of eggs Benedict before Mar and Mindy had gotten up.

As they finished the meal, Ken set his fork across his plate. "How did your niece and nephew like the carousel?"

Mindy blinked several times. "How did you know about that? You must have seen it. But when?"

Ken gave a noncommittal tilt of his head. "Your dad showed me the other night. You ladies were in the kitchen with your mom."

"Susie's face was awestruck. I'll bet that's the way my siblings and I used to stare when he made all those wonderful yard toys for us."

Ken shook his head with a look of bewilderment. "Your dad made that merry-go-round himself? He told me he's going to move it out into the yard when the weather warms up."

Once again, Mar had eaten too much. "If you keep cooking like this, I'm going to weigh a thousand pounds."

"I'm glad you liked it." Ken shrugged. "It's almost easier to cook for a few people than just one."

It didn't seem that way to Mar, but she had an idea and whispered in Mindy's ear. "Top of the Inn?"

"Excellent idea."

Ken crinkled his eyebrows. "What are you two up to?"

Mar stood. "It's a surprise." She hustled into the living room and made her call for a reservation, then returned, zeroing in her focus on Mindy. "Tomorrow night."

Mindy nodded.

"Are you going to clue me in?"

Mar smiled and shook her head. "You'll see."

Ken folded his arms. "What if I'm not available tomorrow night?"

Mindy stood and gathered dishes from the table. "You better clear your calendar, buddy. You don't want to miss this."

Mar helped tidy up the breakfast paraphernalia, then filled Ken in on what had transpired at the nursing home yesterday and their run-in with Dr. Drake.

Ken shook his head. "It's too bad you had such a rough time. I'd hoped you would learn something even though it was Christmas."

"But we did." Mar smiled. "She said we had always been 'beautiful babies.'"

His eyebrows crowded the bridge of his nose. "Why does that help you?"

"Because," Mar continued, "she was talking about the two children born to my mom, not about Mindy. She never saw her as an infant. We can be pretty sure we both survived in order to be 'beautiful babies'. Don't you think?"

Mar's insides danced at the realization of being on the right track. "I think it would be really helpful to have Mom's medical records, but I don't see how we can manage to get them after yesterday's fiasco with Dr. Drake."

Mindy twisted her mouth from side to side. "We can take legal action to get them."

Ken pulled his mouth into a thin line. "I would like to search more in the courthouse archives before we take drastic measures. It's best to save a potential legal battle until we've exhausted all other avenues. The vital statistics records may not have even left the county because they assumed there wouldn't be any follow-up since your mom didn't press the matter at the time. If I don't find anything, we can go to other surrounding counties. I just have a gut feeling about this though, and I think something is out there for us to run across."

Mar suspected he enjoyed a good mystery and the thrill of the hunt. And like a lot of men, he had a drive to fix what seemed to need fixing. In this case, Mar's missing sister. Her enthusiasm soared. "I sure hope either the Swansons or someone else who knew them responds to the ad. This wondering is driving me crazy. I suspect the Swansons might not have any answers about my twin though, because if my mom didn't know where she went, neither would they."

Ken narrowed his eyes as though thinking. "That might be, but if the baby really died, they may know about a grave. We don't want to hear that, but at least you would have answers to your questions. Or they could remember your parents talking about it. Some seemingly insignificant detail could break this case wide open."

Mindy pressed her lips together. "But remember what Mrs. Thomas said about both babies. I'm almost positive we're not going to find a death certificate or anything like that. She wouldn't have been so upset if it wasn't true."

"I can always hope." And Mar's hope could reach to the moon. "I hope she didn't just imagine it." She had to keep her excitement in check.

"Well," Mindy tapped her finger on her chin, "if her imagination had simply run amuck, it wouldn't have upset her to have let something like that slip."

Mar couldn't keep her revelation to herself any longer. "Mindy, remember when she said we had both grown into lovely young ladies?"

Her friend nodded.

"Do you know what that means?" Mar's excitement didn't wait for an answer but bubbled out. "It means she knows who and where my twin is. Otherwise, she wouldn't know she had grown up into a 'lovely young lady.'"

Mindy squealed. "You're right. I never connected those dots."

Mar's elation rose at her friend's confirmation of her assumption. "I wonder how close she lives. I could have nearly crossed paths with her or been at the same event and never even known it."

Mindy's mouth opened in a large 'O'. "Wouldn't it be weird if you walked into a store for the first time and there she was with your face, staring back at you from behind the counter?"

Goose bumps rose on Mar's arms. "Only if we're identical." She couldn't think of any time someone mistook her for someone else.

"Even if you're not, you could look a lot alike." Mindy turned to Ken. "Isn't this wonderful?"

Ken had remained suspiciously quiet. "I suppose." His answer was unenthusiastic, to say the least.

Mar's swirling delight slowed. "What is it?"

He grimaced. "I hate to be a wet blanket."

"But . . .?" Mar wanted to know even if it dashed her dream of finding her sister. She wanted the truth more than anything else. "Spill." If this was all nothing more than an illusion, she didn't want to pursue it.

"We all know how old folks can be." He shrugged. "They get confused and unrelated memories get entwined. To them, they belong together. She could have very well been talking about you and your twin at birth and incorporated Mindy into her thought simply because she was present. So, her compliment might have been for the pair of you. A shift so subtle you missed it. You were overly emotional at the prospect of learning about the past. You might have heard what you wanted to hear."

Mindy sighed. "Oh, Ken, you sound like a lawyer. *And* a wet blanket. Can't you be happy for Mar?"

"I *am* a lawyer, and I *am* happy for her—*if* her twin is real and *if* she's still alive."

Mindy widened her eyes. "But until we know different, let's pretend she's real."

As much as Mar wanted to pretend, it wasn't wise. "No, Mindy. He's right. I am so eager to unpuzzle this mystery, I could be grasping at straws. Concocting a fantasy in my head." She turned to Ken. "Thank you for being the voice of reason." She needed at least one person in this group to keep their feet on the ground.

His tense expression relaxed.

Had he been worried Mar would be angry with him for speaking the truth?

Mindy shifted her attention back to Mar, even slightly turning away from Ken. "Do you suppose Mrs. Thomas said anything to that churlish Dr. Drake after we left?"

Mar smooshed her mouth to one side. "Doubtful. If she did indeed realize she shouldn't have said anything to me, she probably wouldn't confess to him. I wish I could find a way to talk to him, but the likelihood of that is nil. I can't even get in the office door, thanks to Nurse Snippy. She acts as though she's his protector or owns him. Perhaps she has her eye on him and doesn't want anyone else to have a chance."

"Margaret Ross." Mindy's eyes widened in surprise. "You sound as though you have more on your mind than just your mom's medical records. Is the cool, elusive Margaret Ross finally interested in a man?"

Mar's face flushed with heat. "I don't know, Mindy. That just popped out by itself, so maybe I am more interested than I realized. I really do want to get a chance to explain to him that we were only trying to be nice to Mrs. Thomas and perhaps find out something in the process. I wouldn't intentionally intimidate her no matter what I thought she knew." She wanted the good doctor to see she wasn't a bad person. Oddly, his opinion of her mattered.

With a thoughtful expression, Ken rested his chin on his palm. "I've been wondering about Dr. Drake. I'll bet, he hasn't any idea what you're after, Mar. Did you explain to the nurse why your mom's records were important?"

Mar shook her head. "I told her about Mom dying last year and that I needed to find her medical records, but not why. Dr. Drake wasn't her doctor then. She was going to the oncologist. I wonder if that nurse thought I wanted them so I could sue or something."

"You may have hit the nail on the head." Ken raised his eyebrows. "You would think, being a lawyer, I would have thought of that first. I suppose I was more into the mystery than worrying about the way someone else would interpret the inquiry."

"Don't be hard on yourself. You *are* on vacation after all." Mar was pleased to have his help. "Monday, I'll go to his office with a box of candy for Mrs. Thomas. I'll ask him to pass it on as an apology since he doesn't want me to bother her. Then he'll see I'm abiding by his wishes."

Mindy chuckled. "I suppose while you're talking to him, you'll let a bit of the mystery slip out and see if he falls for the bait. Don't forget to mention that you're all alone in the world, and how important it is to find your missing twin."

Ken glanced from one to the other of them. "You two are certainly two halves of a whole, you even think for each other without missing a beat. So, which one of you wants to tell me what's next?"

Mindy gave a smug look. "Mar will bat her big, brown eyes at him, of course, and maybe even conjure a tear or two, but not really cry, and hopefully, he'll agree to hear the whole story."

"I don't think eyelash batting is an effective means to get a person to bend to one's will these days." Mar demonstrated then laughed. "Even if it would work, I can't do it right. I want him to like me and be willing to help, not scare him off. Though, I wouldn't be opposed to asking him out." She held up a hand. "All in the name of acquiring Mom's medical records."

Ken and Mindy exchanged glances and broke out laughing. Mindy recovered first. "You probably would go out with him even if vital information wasn't on the line."

Mar lifted her shoulders. "What can I say? Poor attitude aside, he was handsome. His green eyes sparkled when he was angry with us. I think part of it was his protectiveness of Mrs. Thomas. It showed he's a compassionate man."

Mindy raised her eyebrows. "You noticed an awful lot about him while he was shoving us out the door. I certainly hope, for your sake, he's single."

"Oh, he is." Mar probably shouldn't have answered so quickly. It would give these two more fodder with which to tease her. Too late now. "One of the women I work with at the agency goes to him. She mentioned to some of the other girls about the new handsome, *single*, young doctor in town. I tucked that information in my mental card file for future reference."

She turned to the pair still seated at the table. "Let's go down to Westlake Center to get the candy. That way Ken can see some more of our favorite haunts."

"Marvelous idea." Ken stood. "If I didn't know better, Mar, I'd think you were trying to influence me to move up here someday."

"I probably am." Mar quirked an eyebrow. "Then there will be a better chance of having Mindy around."

Standing, Mindy gave Mar a serious look. "Ken is perfectly happy at the firm he works with now. I don't think he has any intentions to move. You have to put those kinds of ideas out of your mind. I'll try to affiliate myself with a firm in this area though, but I can't make any promises."

Which likely meant she would stay where her heart was. Apparently, part of Mindy's previous "just friends" relationship with Ken had to do with her not planning to stay in California but assuming Ken would. Now that Mindy had faced her feelings for Ken, Mar could see the conflict in her friend's eyes.

Mar swallowed her smile. "I know, but it would be perfect if we were all here in the Puget Sound area." She glanced over at Ken. "I'm sure your sister would agree."

"I'm sure she would." Ken lifted one corner of his mouth. "I'm the only family Jeanne has anywhere nearby. We'll just wait and see what the future brings."

That wasn't a no.

Mar retrieved the jackets from the hall tree. The first stop at Westlake Center was a small café for espressos. Once they were seated, they continued their small talk.

Ken glanced around at the clientele as he finished his drink before them. "Mindy was right about Pacific Northwest people. They basically wear what they want, wherever they want, and whenever they want. She's been telling me for a long time that Northwestern is a lifestyle."

"So true." Mar stood. "You two can wait here while I get the candy if you want."

Mindy groaned as she got up. "I think I'd better move around. I've been sitting too much lately. What about you, Ken?"

He rose too, and the three of them trekked to See's Candies.

Mar entered first. After a candy sample, she purchased a box of assorted chocolate creams for Mrs. Thomas. *Hm. Did Dr. Drake like chocolates? Would a box sweeten up that guard dog?*

Once back at home, the light on her answering machine blinked to indicate a message. Mar listened. "Hello. I'm Lena Bjornson. I'm Rose Swanson's aunt. I saw your ad in the paper." The woman sounded hesitant but left her number. Mar dialed immediately.

After hanging up, she ran into the other room to tell her friends the good news. "Rose Swanson's Aunt Lena called and left a message while we were out. I called her right back. She says Paul and Rose are here in western Washington. They're away this week but will be home on New Year's Day. Maybe it'll be a New Year for me too!"

Please, God, let this new year start with a new family.

Chapter Ten

On Monday, Mar popped the last of her muffin into her mouth and washed it down with the remainder of her coffee. Ken had arrived early and brought the muffins as well as scones and bagels with cream cheese. She brushed the crumbs from her hands. "I'm ready to face my nemesis. How do I look?"

With a tilt of her head, Mindy quirked an eyebrow. "Crush is more like it."

"I can't help it if he's cute." She faced Ken for his assessment and held out her arms in question.

Ken widened his eyes. "Too much girl talk for me, but I'm sure he'll think you look good."

"Thank you." Mar slung her bag over her shoulder. "Wish me luck."

"Of course." Mindy winked. "May the beastly doctor turn out to be your prince charming. Good luck, Mar."

Mar picked up the box of candy and her car keys. *Prince Charming?* She wouldn't mind if he was. *If* his disposition had improved in the last couple of days.

On the way to the clinic, her anxiety over the impending encounter kept quadrupling. *Get a hold of yourself, Mar. You're acting like a puppy who knows it's behaved badly. You haven't acted inappropriately toward Mrs. Thomas. Besides, what's the worst he can do? Throw you out? He's already done that.*

The parking area had only two other cars, so she scored a spot next to the entrance, making for a quick getaway if need be. Clutching the gift-wrapped box, she gingerly approached the outer door with *Dr. Kevin Drake, MD* emblazoned on it, along with *Dr. Jacob Perry, MD*. She gripped the handle and pulled. It didn't budge. She pulled harder. Nope, not opening. Tucking the chocolates under her arm, she cupped her hands around her eyes and peered through the glass. No movement within. Not even the testy red-headed nurse to confront her. The place appeared empty. What should she do now?

As though fulfilling her longing, Dr. Drake strode from around the corner of the building and headed for a silver Lexus.

Thank goodness someone's here. And it's the handsome doctor. With a deep breath, Mar trudged in his direction. "Dr. Drake?"

He glanced up as he unlocked his car. "The office is opening a little late this morning. Dr. Perry will be in around ten."

"I came to see you, to ask you a favor."

He put a leather messenger bag in the back seat. "What can I do for you? I'm technically not at the office today. Just stopped in to get a few things on my way to visit a patient at the hospital, so I hope this is quick." He opened the driver's door.

"Oh, it will be." She focused on talking fast. "I'm Margaret Ross. We sort of met the other day at the nursing home. I was wondering if you would take this gift to Mrs. Thomas next time you go. I would like to assure you that I wasn't trying to frighten her on Christmas. I wanted to give her a small gift and talk to her about my mother. She was all alone and appreciated the company. If I had known you would be visiting, I would have waited until a better time." Stopping to take a breath, she studied him with apprehension.

Dr. Drake stilled and squinted as though confused. "I remember you. Mrs. Thomas is not to be bothered. I have no idea what all this is about your mother. My nurse said you wanted your mother's records. Patty thought perhaps you had the idea Dr. Thomas was responsible in some way for her death. I can't give them to you without the proper paperwork. For all I know, you may not be related to her at all but making false claims."

"Oh. No." Mar gasped. "That's not it at all. Dr. Thomas wasn't my mother's doctor then. She died a little over a year ago from cancer."

"Well then, what is it you think I can help you with?"

Mar's mouth had gone dry and sticky. "I-I really don't know how exactly you could help me." Her voice had an annoying little shake to it. *You have done nothing wrong, Mar.* "You see, Dr. Thomas was my grandparents' doctor, and when Mom found out she was pregnant with me, she went to the Thomases because my grandparents had been killed in an accident. My father was in Vietnam, but the mail got lost or something, so she couldn't ask him for help. That's why she turned to Dr. and Mrs. Thomas."

She halted at his expression of absolute confusion. "I'm not making much sense. I'll begin again, more slowly."

He twisted his wrist, glancing at his watch.

He was likely losing patience with her, so she would talk faster. "You see, I didn't know about any of this myself until just before Christmas when I went to clean out Mom's closet and dresser so I could donate her stuff to the Battered Women's Shelter."

The man appeared to still be at a complete loss as to what she was talking about.

"I'm sorry. You're not following me, are you?"

"No." He shook his head. "I don't see what any of that has to do with your mother's medical records. I really don't have time for a long explanation right now. I'm expected at the hospital."

She had blundered this whole meeting. He would never help her now. Time to cut her losses. "I'm sorry to have taken so much of your time for nothing Dr. Drake." She thrust the wrapped box toward him. "If you wouldn't mind giving these chocolates to Mrs. Thomas when you next see her, I'd appreciate it." With her posture rigid, she turned.

"Miss Ross, I'm not trying to put you off, and I am interested in hearing your story."

Mar spun back in surprise.

Compassion filled his green eyes. "I really am in a rush right now. Can I have Patty make you an appointment? Or I can do it myself later. Would early Wednesday be possible for you? I believe I have some openings then, and it's only a couple of days from now."

"It actually isn't a medical problem, doctor. I would hate to take an appointment from your patients, but then perhaps, you don't have any other time to meet. I don't know why I sounded so confusing. I'm not usually like this at all. Wednesday will be fine, although I don't think your nurse is especially fond of me."

"Since it's not truly a medical issue, maybe it would be easier to talk outside of the office setting . . . Miss Ross."

"Mar."

"Excuse me?"

"Please call me Mar, short for Margaret and a tad more modern."

"Modern Mar, it is." He touched his chest. "Kevin, since we'll be meeting casually outside the office."

A small amount of pleasure swirled inside her. "Kevin's a nice name." *Stupid thing to say.*

He smiled and those green eyes sparkled. "Lunch? Today? That is if you're free. Fewer distractions that way."

"Lunch? Today? Sounds wonderful, Kevin." She couldn't make a worse impression if she tried. "Where shall I meet you? Or you could come to the house if you want, Kevin." Her words were a jumble as well as her brain. And why did she keep repeating his name?

"I feel terrible for snapping at you in the nursing home, so allow me to show you I can be a gentleman and pick you up. How does 11:15 sound? That's when I should be finished at the hospital."

She dug in her bag for one of her cards and handed it to him. "This has both my work and home information on it, but I won't be at work until the Monday after New Year's, so it wouldn't do any good to try me there." She needed to stop blathering.

"Do you like seafood?"

"Do salmon swim upstream? I mean, yes, I love seafood, all kinds."

"Okay then, we can go to one of my favorite places. I'll pick you up at 11:15. I really do need to be getting on." He ducked into his Lexus.

She waved to him. "Goodbye, for now, Kevin."

What had gotten into her? She never acted this vapid. She marched to her car and, despite her inane behavior, practically floated from the parking lot. *Wait 'til I tell Mindy. He actually asked me to lunch.* Turning on her tape player, she sang along with the music all the way home.

Dancing into the house, a self-satisfied smirk on her face, Mar found Mindy on the phone with her mother. She waited impatiently, gesturing for Mindy to hurry. Soon—but not soon enough—Mindy hung up and gave her a playful glare. "What's up that couldn't wait a few minutes? You look like the proverbial cat that swallowed the canary."

"Where's Ken?"

"Snohomish County, doing another search in their records. He thinks he might have missed something."

"Mindy, he's a keeper. Don't let him get away."

"I won't. Now, out with it."

"Oh, Mindy, Dr. Kevin Drake asked me to lunch. Can you believe it? I was so nervous I couldn't make any sense when I tried to explain my predicament to him. Everything just seemed to tumble out all in a mess. He must think I'm a real ditz."

"Take a deep breath, Mar." Mindy led her friend by the arm to the table. "If you'll slow down for a bit, maybe I can determine what it is you're so up in the air about."

"I am up in the air all right. I feel as though I'm walking at least three feet off the ground. I've never felt like this about a guy before. It can't possibly be love at first sight because I don't believe in that. But it's something."

Mindy slapped her hand to her forehead. "No. Not love. Smitten. Infatuated. Crushing. But not love. You're sure not yourself though. Remember your first encounter with him. He *threw you out*. Earth to the real Mar, practical in all things." She gripped Mar's shoulders. "Come back to me."

"Very funny." But Mar felt no humor. "You are no help at all."

"Take a deep breath, start at the beginning, and tell me what happened. If this is the way you were with Dr. Drake, it's no wonder he couldn't understand what you were talking about."

Taking a cleansing breath, Mar recounted the events. "That's when he asked me out to lunch. *Ooooh*, Mindy, he's going to take me to his favorite seafood place. I wonder where it is? What do you think I should wear? And he asked me to call him Kevin, and he's going to call me Mar. He thinks I'm more modern than Margaret." At least she assumed so by his comment.

"Whoa there, buckaroo." Mindy held up a hand. "He obviously doesn't know you too well—the conventional Miss Margaret Ross—or he would never have said that. But if you're going to act like this, he may never realize what a real stick in the mud you can be sometimes."

"All right, I'll try to settle down, but I feel so good about the whole thing. I hope I can get him to help us find some of the answers to the disappearing child. Do you suppose he will?"

"How should I know? He could have talked to you right then. Or invited you for coffee. But he chose lunch. Though it's not a dinner invite, it's still a big deal. I think you ought to take things slow. This needs to be one relationship or the other, either you're wanting him to help in a professional capacity or you're looking for romance. You can't have both. You don't want to mess this up, do you?"

Shock halted Mar. "Why can't he be interested in me *and* want to help me?"

"Maybe he will." Mindy's expression turned worried. "I just think being cautious about when and how you ask him would be prudent. Remember, he's bought that practice from Mrs. Thomas, and he seems protective of her, so if you start making accusations about her and the old doctor, it may not sit well with him. Not on day one, anyhow, before he really knows you. If you want to have a relationship with him in the future, aside from the medical records part, you'd better guard your words in the beginning."

Mar thought for a few moments. "I suppose you're right, as usual. I guess I can't ask one doctor to search for evidence of a crime by another, even if the second one has passed away, at least not until he knows and trusts me. But what reason can I give him for wanting Mom's records? He already knows I want them."

Mindy shrugged. "We'll think of something. What day are you having lunch with him?"

"Today."

Mindy's eyes widened. "So soon? We'll need to think fast."

"You think while I decide what to wear." Mar headed off to her room and gave special attention to her appearance. She needed to make a better impression than she had earlier. She rummaged through her closet from one end to the other and finally took out a softly-fitted suit of golden brown. With it, she chose a warm, yellow-gold blouse. Then to round off the outfit, a pair of low-heeled, leather shoes and a small matching shoulder bag.

Mindy raised her eyebrows. "Wow, don't you look terrific? I see you intend to impress the good doctor, and you certainly should dressed like that."

"I want him to see that there is more to me than the bubble brain he saw this morning."

"You've chosen the outfit to achieve that." Mindy swung on her coat. "If you don't need me anymore, I'm heading home for a bit to help Mom."

"I'll be fine. Tell your mom 'hi' for me."

Mindy waved and left.

Glancing at the kitchen clock, Mar realized she had almost an hour before Kevin would arrive, so she decided to put in a load of laundry and straighten up the living room a bit while she waited. Ken had been keeping the kitchen so clean, that she hardly noticed the rest of the house. After finishing in the living room, she picked up the stack of photos and flipped through them. While most of the snapshots were of all three Rosses, many were also of Mar and Mindy as they grew older. Sighing, she put down the pictures. Why was God's plan for families so different? *Mindy still has her whole family, grandparents and all, but if it weren't for the Stevens, I would have no one.* She sat quietly reflecting on life's twists and turns.

Suddenly, the doorbell rang, startling her. She hurried to open the door.

Kevin Drake stood on the front porch. "Miss Ross—I mean Mar—are you ready to leave?"

He seemed a bit solemn. Had he regretted asking her out?

"Let me grab my bag." Mar snagged it from the kitchen and stepped out onto the porch. "All set."

He held the car door for her before getting in, then headed down across the viaduct into the waterfront area of Seattle.

Mar gazed out the window. Did Kevin's silence mean something was wrong?

He glanced her direction. "If you really don't like seafood, we can go somewhere else. This is just a place I grew fond of when I first moved up here and was interning at Children's. We can go someplace nicer if you'd like."

"I love seafood. I'm not hard to please as restaurants go either. I'm sure I'll love wherever you chose. We could have talked at my house and not gone out if you're pressed for time. I would have understood."

"No." He turned down Pike Street. "I have to eat once in a while, no matter how busy I am, and it will be a pleasure to relax in a favorite spot."

Still feeling apprehensive over his distant demeanor, Mar remained silent.

He parked near Pike's Place Market and led her down a very familiar path to the Greek cafe. Of all the many restaurants in the area, he'd chosen her favorite. Which was also his favorite. Must be a sign that things were meant to be.

Kevin pushed open the etched, stained-glass doors into the big, noisy room. He took her arm, like a chivalrous knight from days of old, and led her toward a raised booth overlooking the Puget Sound. A big ferry boat approached the dock.

Ari skimmed past her with an enormous tray of food. "I'll be with you in a minute, Mar."

She scooted into the booth and noticed a strange expression on Kevin's face. Ari appeared before she had a chance to say a word. He placed two glasses of ice water on the table. "I didn't realize you and Dr. Drake were friends. Where's Mindy and her friend, was it Ken? They haven't gone back to California yet, have they?"

Mar laughed at Ari's inquisitiveness. "No. Dr. Drake and I have just met, and this is kind of a business meeting. I've asked him for help."

Kevin seemed to be studying her and Ari. His eyes squinted slightly. "I thought this was a restaurant, not old home week. Can we have some menus? And come back shortly after we've had time to decide what we would like."

No need for him to be curt.

Ari raised his eyebrows in surprise and opened his mouth to say something, but Mar gave a little shake of her head. She needed the doctor to help her. Ari gave a slight nod and did an about-face.

With a hard expression, Kevin shook his head as he spoke under his breath. "I can't believe this is happening."

Ari returned quickly with two menus, leaving again without a word.

Kevin leaned forward. "Why didn't you tell me you were a regular here? I've been coming about four years now, and I never noticed you before."

Mar took a calming breath and lifted her gaze to his face. "I've never noticed you here either. We probably work different hours and come in on different time frames. Why does it matter anyhow? I didn't realize you meant to bring me to my most loved place for lunch, and by the time I figured it out, we were at the door. It seems we both appreciate this restaurant. It should be something we have in common, not something to be angry about."

Kevin shifted his attention to Ari heading toward them and handed her a menu. "Let's decide quickly what we want so he doesn't have to come back again."

She set the menu on the table without opening it. "I'll have a half-a-crab sandwich and a small Caesar salad, if that's okay."

Kevin's mouth fell open, then he set his jaw. "It's fine." He signaled Ari over. He ordered in a rather curt manner and, when the waiter left, said nothing more.

"You didn't have to order what I like. You should have ordered what you like best."

Kevin widened his eyes in what appeared to be astonishment. "I *did* order what I like. How can you act so innocent? Patty warned me you had probably gone to great lengths to learn all about me, but to go so far as figuring out my favorite restaurant and food is ridiculous! Have you been stalking me?"

Mar snapped with sudden anger but kept her voice perfectly controlled. "How could you even think such a stupid thing? If I hadn't found those diaries and letters last week and needed your help so badly, I would have never gone to your office! I told you I wasn't nurse Patty's favorite person. What makes you think you're so special that I would want to bother?" At the end of her outburst, Mar slid out of the booth. "This was a mistake." With unshed tears and her back rigid, she stumbled across the room and toward the door, bumping into Ari on the way.

The dishes on Ari's tray clinked against each other.

Mar reached out to steady the tray.

"Thanks." Ari's smile faltered.

Mar hurried away and walked blindly down the passage and out one of the rear doors of the public market, she marched up Pike Street for a few minutes, then decided to go to her office and calm down before catching a bus back to west Seattle.

Climbing slowly up the two steep blocks, she put on a smile for the building guard and took the service elevator up to the fourth floor. With everyone off for the holidays, she passed the empty desk in the darkened reception area. Letting herself in with her key, she relocked the door. After washing her face, she took off her jacket and lay on the couch facing the window on the water side of the building.

What a self-centered, self-absorbed egotistical brute. She let more tears stream down her face. She supposed she'd gotten her hopes up too high and too fast. She should have waited until there was no other way to get any information and let Ken ask for it. She knew all the time that the feeling of disappointment had more to do with the attraction she felt for the doctor than the medical records themselves. This was why she didn't date much. She was terrible at picking men.

Well, Mar, you got along without him for nearly thirty years and you can do it again, so pick up the pieces and get on with your life. Slapping away the tears, she stood and glanced out the window. The clouds had grown dark, so she gathered herself up and went downstairs to catch a bus home before rain began to fall.

Mar got off the bus about two blocks from her house. It was colder already and getting dark, so she hustled as quickly as she could without actually running and slipped in the back door.

In the kitchen, Mindy crossed to her immediately with a concerned expression. "What's the matter, Mar? I take it Dr. Drake didn't turn out to be the man of your dreams. Come on, tell me everything."

Mar heaved a huge sigh and slumped into a chair. "I got my hopes up too fast. I'm such a fool."

"We've all been a fool at least once because of a guy."

"Where's Ken?"

"He called. He's on his way. I figured we could get ready to go to Top of the Inn, then we all drive over to his sister's for him to get ready. That is if you still feel like going."

"I left before eating, so I'm starved."

Just as they were almost finished dressing and doing their hair and make-up, the front doorbell rang. Mindy crinkled her brow. "I'll get it. You finish getting ready. It's probably Ken." She hopped on one foot out of the room as she struggled to get her second heel on. Soon, she called, "Mar? He says these are for you."

Mar hurried from her room and found a delivery person on the porch almost hidden behind an enormous bouquet of long-stemmed yellow roses. She drank in the scent of the flowers as she took the card and glanced at it. All it said was "Sorry, Kevin".

She'd only once ever received flowers from a suitor. But Dr. Drake wasn't going to get off that easy. Manners mattered, and he had shown a distinct lack of them. Jumping to conclusions for the second time about her. "Can you please wait a minute? There's been a mistake." She crossed out the original message, turned the card over, and wrote "To Patty, thanks for the advice!" then getting money from her wallet, handed everything to the young man.

His expression turned puzzled. "I don't understand."

"These need to go out to the doctor's clinic near Orchard Park Nursing Home, they're for the nurse, Patty, at Dr. Drake's office."

"All right, if you're sure." He smiled at the generous tip she'd given him and left.

"Margaret Ross!" Mindy planted her hands on her hips. "Why'd you do that? He said they were for you and the card said, 'Sorry, Kevin.'"

"Well, he obviously took his nurse's opinion of me to heart without even meeting me. So, why wouldn't he think to thank her for her advice? It'll serve him right. You weren't with me, and you don't know how rudely he acted. Let him try to explain when she gets the flowers."

"You haven't told me anything, but why would he send those gorgeous roses now if that's how he felt?" Mindy asked. "Was he really rude, Mar?"

"With a capital 'R'. I sure know how to pick them." No more men for her. "Next time I show any interest in the opposite sex, slap me back to my senses."

"You don't mean that."

But she did. The doctor had cured her.

Chapter Eleven

Soon after the flowers had been sent on their way, Ken returned. His expression said he didn't have any luck, then it brightened. "You ladies look lovely."

Mindy did a small twirl. "We are all ready to go to the Top of the Inn."

"You seriously aren't going to tell me anything more than the name of the restaurant?"

With her lips pressed together, Mindy shook her head.

"Judging by the way the two of you are dressed, I'll need to stop by my sister's for better clothes." Ken glanced at Mindy. "Then you can meet my sister and her family."

Mar smiled to herself. Ken was gauging Mindy's reaction to meeting his family.

Mindy didn't disappoint. "That would be great. I would love to meet her. You've talked about her so much."

"Let's go." Ken backed the Chevy down the driveway in the growing darkness and started across the bridge to Kirkland. With the holidays, the light traffic made the trip short.

He pulled up in front of a modern building made of natural wood, set back among the trees. Native plantings added to the beauty of the entry walk. Small crystal lights illuminated the trees and shrubbery, creating a fairyland ambiance.

After putting the vehicle in park, he helped Mindy and Mar out like a true gentleman.

When the front door opened, a tall, slender woman in blue jeans and a ski sweater strolled up the walkway toward them. "Hello, welcome. We've been waiting for you."

Behind her, framed by the light in the doorway, two young children jumped up and down. "Uncle Ken, Uncle Ken, hurry up!"

Still on the outside path, Ken introduced his sister, Jeanne, to Mindy and Mar.

Jeanne hugged Mindy. "I'm so glad to finally meet you. Mar, it's nice to meet you as well. Thanks for having Ken over. It gives him a little time free of the kids."

Ken hurried ahead, grabbing up a child in each arm. He carried them out to meet Mindy and Mar.

Mindy gave them each a hug. "Hi, Bobby and Ashley. I'm Uncle Ken's friend Mindy. He's told me a lot about you. I'm very happy to meet you."

Inside the house, a baby in a playpen had tears running down his rosy cheeks and both hands in the air. "Up, up."

Mar's heart went out to the poor little tyke. "May I?"

"Sure, but he doesn't go to anyone he doesn't know. Not even his uncle yet. So, don't be offended if he rejects you."

Mar folded the little one into her arms, comforting him with gentle pats.

Jeanne stared. "Amazing. I can't believe my little boy let you pick him up. Wait 'til Robert gets here. He won't believe it either."

"Well, he must feel he knows me." Mar swayed with the little one. "Children and babies like me." And if she'd sworn off men, then children weren't in her future either.

Ken shook his head. "You have something I don't. I can't get Josh to even look at me, and here he is cuddled up on your shoulder half asleep already."

Mindy settled on the sofa, about to read a book the other children brought her. "That's true. You should see how much my niece and nephew love her. Sometimes I feel almost jealous, but of course, I love her too."

Mar whispered to not disturb Josh, "You have to remember, Susie and Johnny see me about fifty times to your once, now that you're away at school."

"I don't think it would make any difference." Mindy chuckled. "I guess it's because you play with them like a kid, not like a grown-up."

"Well, whatever it is, it sure works." Jeanne laughed. "If I ever need a babysitter, I know whom to ask."

Ken turned to Jeanne. "I'd better go get cleaned up. They're taking me to someplace called Top of the Inn."

Jeanne's expression softened. "Oh, you'll love it. Robert and I used to go there often before we had this small army. We still choose it for our anniversary every year. What did they tell you about it?"

"We told him how good the food is, especially the seafood, and that he will like the ambiance, but that's all." Mindy made a playful face at Ken. "Our reservation is for 7:30. If you're going to change, you better get a move on."

"Okay." He left the room.

"I'll put him in his crib." Jeanne carefully took the sleeping baby, Josh, from Mar's shoulder, disappeared into the other room, and returned a moment later empty-handed. "Mar, come out to the kitchen while I fix the children's supper plates. Mindy, are you coming?"

Mindy shook her head. "I'll read another story to these two."

"Would you like coffee or anything to drink?"

"I'm fine. Thanks."

Jeanne led Mar into the kitchen. "Ken tells me you three have decided not to go skiing while he and Mindy are here from California."

"I am so sorry for monopolizing all his time while he's supposed to be visiting you. Something came up for me."

Jeanne chuckled. "I think we both know he didn't come all this way because of my squalling brood. You should see the lengths he goes to when deciding what food to make or pick up for you two. One would think it was a major world decision." She rested her hand on Mar's arm. "By the way, I like Mindy."

So, she saw what Mar saw between the pair of lovebirds. "Did he tell you what I'm dealing with?"

"He only said you had a problem, and he and Mindy are trying to help you with it." Jeanne pulled two plastic plates out of the dishwasher. "Is it something you need a lawyer for? If you think I'm being nosy, feel free to tell me it's none of my business."

Mar thought for a minute. "The whole situation has been such a shock to me that I needed Mindy for support. I could hardly wait until she got home, then I found out Ken had come up, and she had promised we would teach him to ski. I was pretty disappointed, but once I met Ken in person, I liked him so much, and he offered to help. It's great having two others to puzzle this all out with."

Jeanne stood at the counter with an expression that could only be described as bewilderment.

Mar halted her rambling. "I'm sorry, Jeanne. I was just rattling on and forgot that you haven't the foggiest idea what I'm talking about." Taking a deep breath, she gave Jeanne the short version. "I want to learn the truth after all these years. It's funny because I keep thinking of her as a baby, but she's nearly thirty, like me." Having run out of steam, Mar released a deep breath.

"Oh." Jeanne blinked several times. "I never imagined a problem like that. I think it's a good thing you have them to help, and I certainly hope you find all the information you're seeking."

Mindy and the children appeared in the doorway. "We've got some tired, hungry kids here. We finished the handful of books in the front room, so I helped them wash up and came in here."

"Thanks so much, Mindy. Apparently, Mar isn't the only one children take to." Jeanne clapped her hands. "Okay guys, hop up on your stools, dinner's ready." She put a plate on the island in front of each child. "Go ahead and eat. Dad will be home soon."

Bobby and Ashley contentedly ate their meal.

Mar and Mindy followed Jeanne into the dining area and sat at the table, each with a cup of coffee in hand now. The room had a glass wall that showcased the lighted evergreen trees and shrubbery, making them appear as though they were almost in the room with them.

Ken entered all shaved, combed, and pink-skinned from his shower. Handsome in his two-piece dark suit with a light blue shirt and a brilliant blue tie with a cream-colored design. It all accented his eyes perfectly.

Mar grinned at him trying so hard to impress Mindy. "My, don't you look spiffy."

Mindy nodded. "*Very* nice."

As the children finished their pudding, the back door opened, and a man she assumed was Robert came in. Ashley and Bobby jumped down and ran over to him. "Daddy."

He picked them up. "Hi, everyone." He crossed to Jeanne and gave her a kiss. "Hi, honey. I didn't know we were having a party."

Ken quickly introduced Mindy and Mar. "It's not a party, Bob. We're going out to dinner. I needed to change into something more appropriate."

Jeanne grinned. "Robert, the girls are taking Ken to the Top of the Inn. I told him it was our favorite place, and that he'll like it as much as we do. I didn't tell him why though."

Robert clasped Ken on the shoulder. "You'll love it."

Mar glanced out the large picture window. "This is such a lovely house. I've never seen one like it."

Jeanne gazed at her husband with pride. "Robert is an architect. He designed it and supervised the construction. It's wonderful to live in. He thought of all kinds of things to make my work easier. I appreciate most of all how he located the laundry near the bedrooms, where most the dirty clothes come from."

"Time for us to go." Mindy crouched in front of the two sleepy children. "We'll see you again soon."

After putting on coats, Mar and her friends walked down the curving path to the car.

Ken drove, and in no time, Mindy directed him to their destination. He squinted up at the Sea-Tac Airport Holiday Inn as he pulled into the hotel's parking lot.

He grimaced as though trying not to say something negative. He might be disappointed now, but in a matter of moments, he would have a whole different opinion.

Mindy wagged her finger. "Didn't you ever learn to not judge a book by its cover?"

Ken helped both Mindy and Mar out. "Sorry. I'm trying not to, but it's human nature."

Mar had been guilty of that with Dr. Drake. Nice packaging on the outside, but churlish on the inside. "Do you trust Mindy's judgment?"

"Of course."

"Then trust her when she says you'll love Top of the Inn."

He took a deep breath as he entered the elevator. "Done. If Mindy loves this place, then so do I."

Right answer. Mar smiled internally.

When the doors opened, *Blue Bayou* surged from the restaurant.

Ken pinched his lips. "This isn't Linda Ronstadt. Whoever recorded this is good."

Mar stepped out into the top-floor lobby and led the way to the restaurant's grand entrance. "Party of three under the name Ross for 7:30."

The host, in a tuxedo, nodded. "Your table is ready. Right this way."

Mar motioned with her hand to Ken. "After you. I don't want to obstruct your first glimpse."

Ken shrugged and forged ahead.

Mar followed into the red and gold lavishly decorated restaurant. Ken stopped short, and Mar bumped into him. In the center of the room sat a grand piano. An apron-clad waitress in a calf-length skirt stood next to it singing.

Ken's mouth hung open. "What is this place?"

Mar held out a hand palm up. "One-part distinctive fine dining." She offered her other hand. "One-part musical extravaganza. And all awesome. Everyone who works here will take their turn singing at the piano. They train singers as waitstaff." She twirled her finger. "This whole platform revolves, making a complete rotation every fifty-seven minutes. You'll get views of the city, Mount Rainier, the Olympics, the airport, as well as a few parking lots and cemeteries."

Mindy urged Ken from behind. "You can gawk from the table. The host is waiting for us."

Ken gave his head a shake and moved in the indicated direction. "Sorry."

The host pulled out a chair for Mar, and Ken held one for Mindy.

Throughout the evening, each waiter, bus person, bartender, and anyone else working there took a turn singing at the grand piano, including their waiter, Calvin.

They had a fresh salad, steamed vegetables, and getting carried away, all ordered lobster. Even though Mar didn't have dessert, she still ate too much. All in all, this had been a fantastic day, even if she hadn't found her twin yet. And even if Dr. Drake had wounded her heart.

Sitting back completely sated, enjoying some after-dinner coffee and watching planes coming and going from the airport, Mar noticed an older lady studying her curiously. She smiled and refocused on her friends.

Five members of the waitstaff descended on the neighboring table and belted out "Celebration" to one of the occupants.

When the song concluded and the singers dispersed, the same lady who had been staring at Mar earlier approached her table. "Marilyn, dear, I wasn't sure it was you. I don't see as well anymore but when you smiled, I was sure, and I wanted to speak to you before I left. I don't mean to intrude on your party, but I'm leaving for Phoenix in a couple of hours. I'll be seeing your folks down there, and I'll be glad to take them a message if you'd like. So many of us have moved south lately. I had to come home for Carolyn though, or I'd still be there too."

Dumbfounded, Mar's mouth almost gaped. "I'm sorry, I can't seem to recall your name." She struggled to place this woman. "But I'm not—"

Mindy kicked her under the table and broke in. "She means she's at a loss for words tonight. I'm sure you'll refresh her memory Mrs.....?"

"I understand, dear." She seated herself in the chair, from which Ken had risen and pulled out for her. "It's Mrs. Iverson. Louise Iverson, your old neighbor from Tacoma. I was surprised to see you. Especially after how devastated you were at the services yesterday over the loss of my granddaughter."

Mindy glanced at Ken. "That's on us, Mrs. Iverson. We couldn't bear to see her so down. What better way to lift a person's spirits than a musical dinner at Top of the Inn? It worked because she's smiling now. Or at least she was."

Mar scrambled to get her brain to catch up, understanding that her friend didn't want her to correct this elderly person. "I'm so sorry about your granddaughter, Mrs. Iverson. I'm afraid it must have been a shock. Is there anything I can do?"

"No, dear, nothing more. Carolyn always loved you so, and just before she passed, when she wasn't able to hold the books she so loved to read by herself any longer, she really appreciated that filigreed book holder you gave her. Books were her one escape. It was good of you to donate several of them in her name to the hospital for use by other patients. Well, I must go now, dear, as my friends are taking me to the airport, and I don't want to keep them waiting any longer." She rose, gave Mar a hug, and strolled out.

Mar stared after her. "That was bizarre."

Ken waved Calvin over. "Bring us your best bottle of champagne. Like the song, we're celebrating."

"Right away, sir."

Dazed, Mar couldn't imagine what he was celebrating. Certainly not the death of that poor woman's granddaughter.

Ken pulled Mar up, giving her a bear hug. He kissed Mindy lightly on the tip of her nose before returning to his seat. "What a break! We can do it now. I'll be off for Tacoma tomorrow. Wherever that is."

Mar blinked several times. "You mind explaining?"

Mindy rolled her eyes. "And you called me dull-witted for not seeing what was right in front of my face. Your twin's name is Marilyn, who used to live in Tacoma. And by the looks of things, she's identical."

The pieces fell into place, and Mar's breath caught with the realization. "Tacoma? She was that close all these years?" She turned to Ken. "It's just down the road from here. We're halfway there already. We can all go, can't we? I couldn't stay at home and wait. We'll do whatever you want us to. We'll be a big help, we promise."

"Of course."

"But I feel bad for misleading that poor woman. I should have told her I wasn't who she thought I was."

Mindy rested her hand on Mar's forearm. "And how long would it have taken to get her to believe you weren't whom she could plainly see with her very eyes you were? If you did remotely convince her, she would have been questioning it all the way home on her flight. Let her have this peace. She apparently just buried her granddaughter."

Mindy was right, of course.

Calvin appeared with the champagne in a silver bucket, steaming from the cold ice, and three fluted glasses. He removed the bottle with his white-gloved hands and showed it to Ken. "For your approval."

Ken studied the label for a few seconds and nodded.

Their waiter removed the foil and gripped the neck of the bottle.

Mar cringed, hoping the cork wouldn't go flying.

But the waiter placed his thumb over the cork and twisted the tab on the wire cage several times.

She supposed that was smart.

He moved the napkin from his arm and covered the cork, careful to replace his thumb. With the bottle at a forty-five-degree angle, he turned the bottle until the champagne whispered a sigh of effervescence.

She sighed as well at the expertly executed task.

He set the cork aside.

Now, with one glass also at a forty-five-degree angle, he poured about an ounce and offered it to Ken.

Ken sniffed and took a sip, then nodded.

Calvin topped off his glass, then poured a glass each for Mar and Mindy, before returning the bottle to the ice bucket and departing.

Ken raised his glass. "To success."

Mar and Mindy echoed his words and clinked their glasses with his. Not only was there bubbly in Mar's glass, but her whole inside was bubbling with excitement. Her sister—*Marilyn*—was within reach.

Chapter Twelve

Just before midnight, Ken dropped Mar and Mindy off at her house. Like a gentleman, he waited until they were inside before pulling away. Mindy gazed out the window long after he was gone.

Would Mar ever have a love like that?

The phone rang, causing Mar to nearly jump out of her skin.

Mindy spun around. "Who would be calling at this hour?"

It was never good. Mar snatched up the receiver.

"This is the Harborview emergency room. I have a Mrs. Littlefoot here. She's asking for you to transport her to the women's shelter."

"Yes, I'll be there in about half an hour." Mar hung up. "I need to take someone from the hospital to the women's shelter. There's no one else available tonight."

"Do you want me to go with you?"

Mar waved her friend off. "I'll be fine. I've done this lots of times before. But I'd better have a cup of coffee and be on my way."

Mindy shooed her. "I'll make the coffee while you change out of your fancy duds."

Mar glanced down at her little black dress and strappy heels. "Good idea."

When she returned to the kitchen in a baggy sweatshirt and jeans, Mindy handed her a hot cup of coffee with a rapidly melting ice cube in it. Mar appreciated her friend thinking to cool the coffee. In a few gulps, she finished the caffeinated beverage, picked up her keys from the counter, and dashed out.

After parking at Harborview, Mar locked the car and entered through the emergency room doors. She approached the desk.

"Oh, Miss Ross, you're here." Mrs. Martin, the attendant with whom she was well acquainted from previous visits, sounded almost grateful. "It's Betsy Littlefoot again, and when I told her no one was available, she begged me to have someone call you. She insists you'll take her and that you'll understand. I told her one of the social workers could be called, but she only wanted you. Is it all right? The people at the shelter said you'd be happy to help, but I hated to bother you at this time of night."

"It's okay, Mrs. Martin. I was still up. We just got home from a night out. I'm really disappointed about Betsy, though. I was hoping the situation was under control. I won't say that to her though. She loves her husband, and he's a wonderful father and mostly a good husband. He's been more than willing to go to all the counseling and alcohol sessions, but once in a while that devil drink *John Barleycorn* gets the best of him, and this is the result. We'll all keep praying and hope for the best."

"Will you go in and talk to her, Miss Ross? She's waiting for you to get here even though the doctor is still stitching her up. It won't bother you to see that will it?" Without waiting for an answer, she headed for an area at the far end of the room.

Following, Mar saw the young mother lying on an ER bed. The doctor sat on a rolly-stool bent over her leg with his back to Mar. Betsy looked up and broke into a big grin. "Oh, Miss Ross, I knew you'd come. Thank you for being my friend. Nurse Martin wanted to call a social worker, but I said 'no,' I wanted you."

"It's okay, Betsy. Just be still until the doctor is finished with you, then we'll do whatever you need. I'm sure the shelter is the best thing for now."

"It'll only be for a few hours, then Johnny will be off on a lumber run, and we can all go home."

"Are the children all right?" Mar prayed the man hadn't injured any of them as well.

"They're fine, Miss Ross. My mom has them, but they're bigger now. Johnny wouldn't ever hurt them anyhow, you know."

"I'm sure you're right, Betsy." Mar had never heard of a time when he had, but there could always be a first. She took Betsy's hand. "I'll be right here with you, so just relax for the doctor."

The doctor seemed a bit stiff and oddly quiet. He probably feared Mar would interfere with what he was doing. He needn't worry. Mar's only concern was Betsy.

Finishing with the leg but keeping turned away from Mar, he touched the area around Betsy's eye. He picked up a gauze pad, and covering it with salve, taped it solidly to her skin. "There, Mrs. Littlefoot." He spoke in a hushed voice. "I think that will do for now. Make an appointment at my office next week."

"Sure, Dr. Drake. Thanks for fixing me up."

Mar froze. *Dr. Drake?* What was he doing here? Of course, as a doctor, why wouldn't he be here? She hadn't expected to see him again this soon.

Had he learned what she'd done with the roses yet?

Rising and turning in what seemed a single motion, Dr. Kevin Drake stood, looking down at Mar. "Well, Miss Margaret Ross, it seems as though everyone I know is also acquainted with you. May we speak alone for a minute? Will that be okay, Mrs. Littlefoot? I'll let her come right back."

"Sure, Dr. Drake." Betsy turned her concerned expression to Mar.

Mar gave the woman a reassuring nod.

Dr. Drake motioned her toward the door and let her lead the way into the hall.

Once out of the room, Mar stopped and folded her arms, waiting silently for him to make the next move.

He studied her a moment before speaking. "I want to tell you about the lovely roses my office nurse received earlier. That was a little bit poisonous. How did a nice girl like you decide to make a move like that?"

Mar locked her gaze with his. "It just came to me like a bolt out of the blue. I realized your nurse, Patty, had taken an instant dislike to me, so I was pretty sure she was the root of your prejudice toward me. It seemed only fair to share the spoils with her. Did she like them?" Mar could have sent them to the nursing home for someone's birthday or the women's shelter to be enjoyed, but she had allowed her devious nature to take over. And she wasn't going to apologize.

"She did, but I'm afraid you've given her ideas about me."

"My guess is she already had those ideas."

"It seems that the people we have in common have very high opinions of you. I really am trying to apologize, Miss Ross. I was a rude and obnoxious boor who jumped to conclusions without waiting to form my own opinion. I wish we'd met under better circumstances. Will you please forgive me?"

"You're forgiven. I guess we're even now. One thing I want to make clear, though, is that if you intend to get to know me, you either like me or dislike me on my own merits. Not someone else's pre-formed opinion."

"That's fair."

"If that's all, I would like to get back to Betsy."

He nodded and followed her into the exam room.

The woman lay sleeping, slightly snoring.

The doctor studied Betsy's chart for a moment before setting it back down. "She needs to be monitored by the ER staff for at least a half hour. May I interest you in lukewarm hospital coffee in a Styrofoam cup, Miss Ross?"

"Sounds enticing." Mar walked to the coffee machine with him, then sat in the waiting room. Surprisingly, the time flew by with small talk and getting to know a few things about each other. "If it's been long enough, I would like to take Betsy to the shelter for the rest of the night."

Kevin threw their cups away. "Would you allow me another chance to have lunch with you?"

"That would be nice."

"Wednesday's my day off. Perhaps we should go someplace where we're a little less well-known. I can pick you up at the same time. How about going out to Hiram's at the Locks? We can watch the boats ride up and down. I promise to be nicer."

Mar smiled, nodding. "The locks are great, even in winter." Now, she wished she'd taken more care in her attire, but how was she to know she would run into the handsome doctor.

Kevin helped her wake up Betsy and walked the pair to the emergency room exit before being paged to handle another crisis. "Ah," he sighed to himself. "I knew it was too good to last." He dashed back inside.

Mar dropped Betsy off, handing her over to the shelter personnel. "If you need me for anything, Betsy, you call me yourself. You don't have to depend on others to reach me. I'm truly your friend, you know, and please remember to call me Mar."

"Okay Miss R . . . er Mar, it just seems we come from two different worlds, and I should be respectful."

"Oh, Betsy." Mar gave her a careful hug so as not to hurt any of her injuries. "We may have come from two different worlds, but we've met in this one and become dear to each other. We live in this world, both of us together. If you want or need anything, you call me yourself."

By the time Mar arrived home, her bedside clock read nearly three a.m. Groaning and closing her eyes, she recalled the events of the past twenty-four hours. What an unexpected roller-coaster today had been—or rather yesterday. She snuggled in, knowing she wouldn't get much sleep before she needed to rise and shine.

Sometime later, Mar rolled over and forced one eye open. Light filled the room, and her clock read ten a.m. *Oh, no.* She sprang out of bed. Hopefully, Mindy and Ken hadn't left her behind.

Swinging on her robe, she raced to the kitchen where Ken and Mindy sat at the table, reading the morning paper like an old married couple. "I was afraid you had gone without me."

Mindy stood, poured a cup of coffee, and handed it to Mar. "You came in so late, I didn't want to wake you. We figured we would let you sleep until you got up on your own and then we would head down to Tacoma. This is your rodeo. We wouldn't dream of going without you."

"Thanks." Mar sipped her coffee. "You two are the best."

Ken held a large bakery box open from the local grocery store. "Decided a quick and easy breakfast for today would be best."

Mar snagged a maple bar and a blueberry muffin.

"Would you like a glass of grapefruit juice to go with that?"

"Fresh squeezed?"

Ken chuckled. "Sorry. Fresh bought this morning."

"I guess it will have to do." Mar winked and sat. She took a bite of the sweet, heavenly pastry. "Do you really believe this girl named Marilyn could be my missing twin? I so desperately want it to be the case that I'm willing to believe most anything."

Mindy sat back down. "Are you kidding? She's your *identical* twin. Mrs. Iverson didn't hesitate once she got close enough to see you clearly. She apparently lived next door to her most of her life. If there were any real differences between you two, she would have realized her mistake as soon as she got up to the table. Instead, she settled right in when Ken offered her a chair. She actually got closer and hugged you, sure that she was embracing Marilyn."

"I hope you're right." Mar felt more confident with her friends' assurances.

Mindy flipped open a spiral notebook. "We cross-referenced our Brower's Funeral Home information with Dr. Thomas's obituary again.

Like at the cemetery, we found no offspring for Dr. and Mrs. Thomas, so our assumption they never had children is likely accurate. Ruth Gordon was listed as a niece. Ruth lived or had been living in Tacoma at the time of the doctor's death. We're definitely on the right track now."

Ken tapped the notebook. "If we can match up the Gordons from Tacoma with a Louise Iverson from the same, I'll feel positive myself that Marilyn is the right girl."

When Mar had finished eating, she took a shower and got ready for a day of discovery. She returned to the kitchen.

Mindy stood at the window. "It may be a gray day in Seattle, but it's beginning to feel like a good day down the road in Tacoma. At least that's what my woman's intuition is telling me."

Mar laughed. "Mindy, you know that saying women have intuition and men don't is a chauvinistic thing. Remember you're a lawyer, or almost anyway."

Mindy spun around and held one hand up. "Women have intuition." She lifted the other. "Men have gut feelings."

"What's the difference?"

Mindy shrugged. "The spelling."

Mar rolled her eyes and shook her head then filled her cup before sitting down. "Any new breakthroughs while you two were out here unchaperoned?"

Ken grinned. "At our age, unchaperoned is a relative term. We've passed the need for that. Now we should just get married and get on with life." He turned to Mindy. "Will you tell her, or shall I?"

"I don't know if either of us should tell her after that remark about intuition. Maybe we should reconsider."

"Oh, come on, Mindy, you knew all the time it was a joke."

"Okay, I'll talk." Mindy beamed. "We were wondering if your birthday will be a good day. What do you think?"

"How would I know what kind of day it'll be? It's nearly six months away." Mar gave a wry smile.

Ken's expression turned confused. "Mindy means for the wedding, Mar, our wedding."

Mar widened her eyes in mock surprise. "We're getting married, Ken? Does Mindy know?"

Ken furrowed his brow. "No, I mean Mi—"

Mindy broke in laughing. "Don't bother, Ken. She knew from the very first word and maybe even before that exactly what we were talking about. Didn't you, Mar?"

Mar laughed. "But I thought Ken just said *we* were getting married. Isn't that what you said, Ken?"

Looking from one to the other, Ken laughed too. "I should be used to the two of you by now. I suppose it's the lawyer in me that lets me fall for it every time. Yes, Mar, we're getting married. All three of us, she is going to be part of it, isn't she, Mindy? I thought you told me if she behaves herself, she can be the old maid of honor."

"Ouch. I deserved that." Mar put her mug in the sink and headed for the door. "On the way, I'll fill you in on what happened at the hospital last night."

"Um." Ken's expression turned worried. "You shouldn't be sharing confidential patient information with us."

"Oh, I'm not sharing patient information. I'm sharing doctor information. The ER doctor was none other than Dr. Kevin Drake. And let me tell you, he was as surprised to see me as I was him." But she was so glad to have smoothed things over with him.

Chapter Thirteen

On the drive to Tacoma, with high hopes of finding much more information in the city to the south, Mar told her friends about all that transpired during her most recent encounter with Dr. Drake. "I have mixed feelings about having lunch with him. A part of me longs for another chance at a date. But another part wonders if it is such a good idea." She clearly understood what Mindy had been trying to warn her about in having a dating relationship or a business one.

Mindy nodded. "Tread lightly and see how things go. And by all means, keep your expectations low. I don't want him to hurt you again."

"Don't worry. I'll be careful." She had learned her lesson. Right now, it was more important to find her sister than begin a romance.

Ken turned the conversation to earlier the night before. "You know, when you two wanted to take me out to dinner at a special place, I was surprised it wasn't the Space Needle." He merged onto I-5. "I couldn't imagine how anyplace could be as notable as I've heard it is. However, after we got to the restaurant, I understood your excitement about the Top of the Inn. What a great experience. I want to go again when I can anticipate the evening for a while first."

Mindy smiled. "I knew you'd love it. You appreciate good music and excellent food. Now, you have a place where you can find both. Wasn't our waiter fun? He sure had a wonderful voice, and it's great he's studying opera."

"He'll probably make it too." Mar's nerves were sizzling, but she tried to focus on the conversation rather than what might or might not unfold today. "He's a handsome guy and opera-size, as we could all see."

"Don't worry about the Space Needle, Ken." Mindy touched his forearm. "My folks have reservations for New Year's Eve. They made them almost a year ago. They've made allowances for plus ones, so you're welcome too."

"I look forward to it." Ken inclined his head.

Nearing what she hoped would be their destination, Mar pointed to a road sign. "One mile until the exit we need."

Mindy twisted to face Mar in the back. "I'm sorry. We forgot to tell you. We decided we should go to the records department first in case they close early due to the holidays. So we should bypass that exit and take the 38th Street one." She tapped the map she held in her lap.

In a few minutes, Ken took the proper turn and soon found the Pierce County Annex. Trooping into the building with her friends, Mar requested property information and was sent to the auditor's office down the hall.

After securing Marilyn's old address, Mar headed toward the exit with her friends.

Ken slowed his pace. "I should ask about birth and adoption records while we're here." Upon making inquiries, he was directed to the Pierce County Health Department on Pacific Avenue, as it was the place to obtain those kinds of documents.

A smattering of tiny waterdrops speckled the car.

Ken pointed to the windshield. "It rained while we were in there."

"Nah." Mar waved her hand at the Chevy. "A momentary drizzle."

Sitting inside on the front seat, Mindy unfolded and consulted the city map. "It's actually sort of on the way to the Gordons' old neighborhood. Just a hop, skip, and a jump over a few streets."

The trip was quick. With minimal traffic. Once there, Ken got out. "I'll be right back."

Mar exchanged a glance with Mindy. "What are the chances he *will* 'be right back'?"

Mindy heaved a sigh. "These things always take longer than we expect."

"My thought exactly." Mar pointed down the street. "There's a coffee shop. Let's get lattes." She opened her door and scrambled out.

Mindy climbed out too.

At the shop, Mar and Mindy each ordered their drink, and Mindy ordered a second one. She glanced at Mar. "For Ken."

"You know it'll likely be cold before he's done in there?"

"Yes, but he'll know we were thinking of him."

Once they had their lattes in hand, they trekked back to the Chevy. Ken sat in the driver's seat. He got out. "I thought you ladies had abandoned me."

Mindy held the second cup aloft. "We brought you sustenance."

Mar exchanged another glance with Mindy acknowledging the insightful decision to get him one too. Then she turned to Ken. "Was it a bust? Is that why you returned so quickly?"

"On the contrary." With a broad grin, he waved a paper at Mar. "Here's the proof we needed, so let's get going."

Mar snatched the paper. She couldn't believe it. Marilyn's birth certificate. "Oh Ken, how did you find this so fast?"

Mindy peered over her shoulder.

Ken tapped his head. "I used my noggin for a change. I flashed my business card and simply asked for Marilyn Gordon's birth certificate, giving your birth date. And voila, I held the long-sought paper in my hand. I must confess I didn't act much like a dignified young lawyer when I practically ran to the parking lot and let out a whoop of delight. And what surprise awaited me? You two were gone."

Mar raised her hand. "My fault. I thought it would take longer." She returned her focus to the document. "If we'd found this first, it would have been so much easier. Here's her name, parents', and it's signed by Dr. Thomas. The only thing different is the place of birth. It doesn't say she was adopted but rather a 'live birth.'"

"Which supports our theory about the Thomases giving the baby to someone else. In this case, their own niece. That is if she is indeed your twin. So far, all our evidence supports that theory."

Mar rubbed her hands together. "Now that we're making progress, let's see what we can dig up at the Gordons' old house. If we have time enough after, maybe we can stop by the hospital and ask a few questions about Mrs. Iverson's granddaughter. That could shed some light on this as well."

Her insides warmed with happiness and satisfaction.

Ken drove down the long hill and up again into the historic section of town with stately homes. Old-fashioned lamps lined the road with the promise to flicker on when it got dark. Beautiful, large yards filled with shrubbery and some statuary unfolded before Mar as she watched for the house her twin grew up in.

Nearing a large corner lot, Ken pulled to a stop at the curb.

Mar's breath caught. *This is it.*

"What a grand house." Mindy tilted her head and looked up through the car window at the three-story white home surrounded by hedges. "How could anyone have sold this beauty?"

A separate garage with stairs leading to the second floor appeared to have an apartment above it. It had likely once been a carriage house in bygone days. With the heavy clouds overhead, the Christmas lights were visible, glowing on the trees, shrubs, hedges, and all the roof lines of the grand manor. They gave the illusion of a fairyland.

"It's so heavenly," Mar breathed the words wistfully. "I wish we could just knock and have Marilyn open the door."

"Since her family no longer owns the house, that's unlikely." Mindy exited the car. "But it can't hurt to knock. Maybe the person who lives here now knows something."

Mar scrambled out, followed by Ken.

As Mar climbed the steps to the columned porch and its heavy, carved oak door, the holiday lights under the overhang sparkled on the oval etched glass. Her knees threatened to give way. "You guys need to hold onto me." Such a different home to grow up in than Mar had. Trembling slightly, she pressed the doorbell. Musical chimes echoed through the house. She almost didn't dare to breathe. A door closed somewhere in the upper regions of the house and footsteps descended the stairs.

Soon, the front door opened, revealing a well-dressed woman, not much older than Mar and her friends. "Hello, may I help you?"

Mar's voice croaked, so she cleared her throat. "Hello, we're old friends of the Gordons. We went to college with Marilyn and were hoping to find out where she is now." *Please don't slam the door on us.*

The woman's face broke into a welcoming smile. "How sweet of you to look up an old school chum. I'm Shelly Hanson. We've lived here less than a year, and this place was empty when we bought it. We never met the Gordons. Everything was handled by the real estate company and the Gordons' lawyer. I was told they'd already moved south. Arizona or New Mexico if I remember right. Come in out of the cold, and we'll try to find some answers for you." Stepping back, she gestured for them to enter.

"Thank you." As Mar crossed into the entry with its wide, curving staircase and grandfather clock, she felt as though she'd stepped into another world. Being invited in was better than she had hoped.

Mindy gazed upward. "I can't imagine how they could let such a lovely house go out of the family."

"We wondered about that too." Shelly closed the door. "But the real estate agent said Mr. Gordon's doctor recommended the move to a dryer climate. She also told us they have only one child who didn't live with them any longer. I think she works out of the country, at least part of the time."

Mar's hopes deflated. Marilyn didn't even live in the area? Or the country? It would be harder to locate her and take longer before she could meet her.

Mrs. Hanson led them into a room off the hall. "Have a seat, and I'll call my neighbor who has lived here almost forever and see if she has their contact information." She headed for another room.

Sitting cautiously on one of the loveseats flanking the fireplace, Mar glanced around at the beautifully carved oak mantelpiece and the many bookshelves lining the walls. "I wouldn't have minded growing up in a house like this myself. Not that I would've given up my folks for anything, but this sure is terrific."

"I wouldn't mind living here right now." Mindy gazed at Ken, wiggling her eyebrows.

Mrs. Hanson returned with disappointment etched on her face. "I'm afraid my friend wasn't as much help as I'd hoped, but she did confirm that it was Phoenix they moved to. She thinks she got a Christmas card from them, and if she can find the envelope with the return address, she'll call me. Leave your number so if I get it or any other news, I'll be able to reach you."

Mar sighed. "She didn't know anything about Marilyn then, I guess."

"Well, she knew that the daughter works for a major overseas airline, although she couldn't remember which one."

Ken spoke up for the first time. "We know she was here in Tacoma for some time recently since her friend Carolyn Iverson was in the hospital. The Iversons were old neighbors of the Gordons."

"Yes." Shelly Hanson nodded. "I read of her death in the paper a few days ago. Cancer. She was so young."

"I'm sure it was tragic for all of them." Ken nodded. "We saw her grandmother at dinner last night. Apparently, Marilyn had visited Carolyn every day at the end and often before that."

"We mustn't keep you from what you were doing." Mar rose from the loveseat. "Thank you for talking with us. Here's my card. You can reach me at either home or work—after the first of the year—if you find out anything you think might help us."

"Oh, I was just finishing up some tag ends of Christmas chores." She waved off the concern. "It was nice to hear the doorbell ring for a change. I work a lot, and my husband is often out of town, so we haven't made too many friends since being transferred here from Ohio."

"Just you and your husband live here?" Mindy's gaze wandered the scope of the room. "It seems like a place that cries for a big family. I'm sorry, I didn't mean that, it just popped out."

Shelly beamed. "That's why we bought it. Up 'til now, I've been focused on my career, but now it's secure, and we hope to start having babies. We both come from large families and want to have at least three of our own." She led them to the entry hall.

Mar slowed. "Um. Ever since I've known Marilyn, I've been dying to see her stately home. Would it be too much to ask for a quick tour of the house? If not, I totally understand."

"Of course. We're not finished decorating yet, but I inherited some wonderful antiques from my grandmother. Then coming from Ohio, Civil War country, I've added to them not knowing if we'd ever have a home for them. This one is just perfect." She led the way upstairs and down, imparting what history she knew.

When the enjoyable tour ended, Mar thanked her graciously and stood near the front door. She wanted to linger and soak in where her twin had grown up. She felt a connection to Marilyn here. Walking where she had walked. Trying to guess which room might have been hers.

Shelly stood on the porch waving. "Try contacting your old school office. Marilyn may have left an address for reunions and events."

"Thanks." Mar waved back before climbing into the car.

Ken drove toward the middle of town.

Mar sighed. "Well, this day sure has been filled with ups and downs. We learned a lot, however, some answers still elude us. But as my mom used to say, 'perseverance wins.'" That was certainly the case today and since learning of her twin.

Chapter Fourteen

After the tour of Marilyn's childhood home, Mar's hopes sailed higher than ever. She was so close to finding her sister, she could practically see her. She giggled to herself. All she had to do was face a mirror to glimpse her identical twin.

"Are we still stopping at the hospital?" Ken turned out of Marilyn's old neighborhood. "It might start drizzling again."

Mar glanced out the window at the cloudy sky. "No. These clouds aren't going to produce any more rain." Even if they did, it wouldn't dampen her mood.

"How can you tell? They look like rain clouds to me." Ken seriously needed to grow some webbed feet. Fairweather people could be so funny about rain. In middle school, the baseball team was released from classes to bail out the diamond—*while* it was *still* raining.

"We're almost at the hospital already." Mar pointed. "In fact, if we turn here and go up a couple of blocks, we'll be at the Tacoma hospital. It makes sense for that to be the one Carolyn had been at. I just want to run in and see if any of the nurses who knew Carolyn are on duty. Perhaps someone will remember Marilyn."

In a few minutes, Ken pulled into the parking lot. "Here we are."

Mar opened her door. "You guys can stay in the car. I'll be right back." She hurried in before either of her friends could delay her.

Being a different hospital than she usually went to, she stopped at the reception desk and told the attendant she needed to know what floor her best friend Carolyn had been on. "I want to let the nurses know I appreciate the great care they gave her."

She thanked the lady for directions and hurried down the corridors, following the proper color lines until she stood in front of the nurse's station. A young nurse with freckles, blue eyes, and short, curly, light brown hair stood there writing on a chart. When the woman looked up from her task, she smiled widely and, before Mar could say anything, came around the end of the counter and gave her a hug. Surprised, Mar opened her mouth to speak but didn't know what to say.

"Marilyn," the nurse said. "How come you're back again so soon? I didn't expect to see you for a long time. You took so much time off when Carolyn was here. I was expecting a postcard from one of those exotic places you fly to."

This woman obviously knew Mar's twin and remembered Carolyn. "You're one of the nurses who took care of her, aren't you?"

"Marilyn. You know I am. I took extra shifts to be with her. What's gotten into you? Why are you acting weird?"

With a sinking feeling, Mar knew she couldn't pretend to be Marilyn this time, not with someone who knew her as well as this nurse seemed to. Gathering up her courage, she took a deep breath. "I'm not Marilyn. My name is Margaret Ross. I've come because I hoped someone might be able to help me find her. I learned about Marilyn just before Christmas, and I've been trying to find her ever since. It's a long story."

With a dumbfounded expression, the nurse stepped back and surveyed Mar from head to toe. "You are being honest with me, aren't you? I could swear you're Marilyn trying to pull a trick on me. Other than how you're dressed and your hair a little different, you're the spitting image."

"No, no trick." Mar shrugged one shoulder. "You seem to know Marilyn well. I'd like to learn more about her if you have time."

The woman shook her head. "No, Marilyn. We've been friends since grade school. I know it's you. You can stop the act."

This was all a bit too much to believe. Mar pulled out her wallet and removed her driver's license. "See? Margaret Ross."

She studied the ID with wide eyes. "I-I-I . . ." She paced the corridor back and forth a couple of times. "I can't believe this."

"It is pretty incredible."

The nurse halted and put her hand on her chest. "I'm Diane Oliphant. Wait here a minute while I'll make sure there aren't any emergencies to attend to, then we can have coffee and talk."

In a few minutes, she returned, holding two mugs. "Let's sit in the nurse's lounge where we'll be more comfortable. I've asked another nurse to cover for me."

Mar settled into a padded chair next to Diane. She told of finding her mother's papers and other things, then ended by relating about acquiring Marilyn's birth certificate, locating the Gordons' old home, and the visit with Shelly Hanson.

Diane rose and walked the length of the room a couple of times. "I've known Marilyn since we were ten years old, and we've always confided in each other everything. She never said anything about the Gordons not being her natural parents or that she could possibly have an identical twin or any other sibling. This is serious." She stopped on the far side of the room and seemingly stared at the wall for nearly a minute.

Should Mar say something? Or remain quiet to let her sort this out in her own head?

Diane made the return trip. "She needs to be told *and* in person in a gentle way. Do you think someone could talk to her parents and somehow persuade them to be honest with her? I could tell you how to reach her, but I really don't want to at this point. I think we should go through the Gordons first. If they don't cooperate, then we'll rethink what to do. Or is it so imperative that you can't stand to wait any longer?"

It was refreshing to have Diane believe her and be willing to help. "Of course, I feel anxious to find her and resolve this mystery. I certainly understand the rationale for doing as you suggest. My head says we should go slowly, but my heart says 'hurry, hurry.' It tells me that somewhere out there is a person so much a part of me that we belong to each other, and every minute apart is a great loss for both of us."

Diane wrapped her arms around Mar. "I understand how you feel and your need to get this settled, for your sake and Marilyn's. Let me think on it. She's on a charter and unreachable at the moment. I can meet you later today after my shift. Can we get together then and decide what, when, and how to go about telling her and her parents? It'll also give us a chance to get to know each other better."

"That would be wonderful." Preparing to leave, Mar retrieved one of her business cards with her phone numbers and address, made a note on it, and thanked her new-found friend. "Oh, Diane, I'm so glad I discovered you. I feel as though my search will soon be over."

Diane accepted the card. "So, you've been trying to figure this out all alone? You could stay at my place tonight, and we could get to know each other. It will be interesting to figure out how you are different from her."

"Alone? I'm not alone. My two friends are waiting for me in the car." Mar widened her eyes. "Oh my gosh, I forgot about them. Diane, call me at home later or just come on over. Thanks for everything. Mindy's gonna kill me!" She dashed off to find her friends. In her rush, she didn't follow the correct-color lines. Eventually, she wound her way back to the main lobby where Mindy and Ken stood, watching the big fish tank.

"Finally! We got tired of waiting in the car." Mindy burst out. "If this is your idea of right back, I'd hate to 'wait a little while' for you. You'd better have a good story cuz we're famished."

"Boy, do I." Mar led the way to the exit. "But let's get something to eat first. All of a sudden, I'm starving too. The world-famous Frisko Freeze is only up the block."

Ken pulled into the small parking lot. "Is this just a drive-thru?"

"Frisko is not *just* a drive-thru. It's an experience—and also has a walk-up order window, so go ahead and park. Then tell me what you all want, and I'll get it. My treat after making you guys wait."

Fifteen minutes later, Mar returned to the car with a tray loaded down with hamburgers, fries, and shakes. After several minutes of silence from the hungry crew, Mar launched into meeting Diane and who she was. "I can't believe how I simply walked in, and Marilyn's friend recognized me. As close as we were, she still thought I was her pal playing a trick on her."

Ken crumpled the empty wrapper from his burger. "How do you feel about contacting the Gordons so they can tell Marilyn themselves?"

"Okay, I guess." She retrieved a fry. "I hate having to wait, but I know Marilyn isn't available, so I would have to wait anyhow. If I were in her place, I would rather hear it from my folks than a stranger." Even if that stranger was her twin. She popped the salty potato into her mouth.

Mindy wedged her shake between the dashboard and the windshield. "While you were out getting the food, Ken said if you felt more comfortable not talking to the Gordons yourself, he would be happy to fly to Phoenix on your behalf. It might be easier for them if the information came from a lawyer. More impersonal anyhow."

"Let's think about it. Diane will come over later today after she's off. Let's see what she thinks of Ken's offer. It would be less traumatic for her parents, and Diane knows them best. We can all hash out a plan then."

Ken sucked down the last of his shake. "What's with this hamburger place? I've never had anything like it before. It's not a chain, is it? How did you even discover it?"

Mar laughed. "Frisko Freeze is so famous and popular around here that our governor has his driver take him here for lunch anytime he's in Tacoma."

"It was terrific and different too." He groaned and patted his stomach. "Everywhere you gals take me for food is special. If it doesn't stop soon, I won't be able to get into my car when I have to go back to work."

"You know what this means?" Mindy spoke a little slow as though deep in thought.

Though normally able to read her friend's mind, Mar's brain was still trying to sort out all the new information she'd received in the past nine days. "Can you be a bit more specific? A lot has transpired today."

"In light of learning your twin's name, her parents' names, acquiring her birth certificate, where she lived, and finding her best friend, we may not need your mom's medical records nor Dr. Drake."

No Dr. Drake? How disappointing. "There could be something in them we haven't thought of yet. Maybe?" She'd just made up with the man. He deserved a second chance.

Ken shrugged. "It couldn't hurt."

Mindy's expression turned shocked. "He could stomp all over her feelings again."

Ken tilted his head toward Mar in the backseat. "She has a point."

"Mindy, I appreciate your concern, but I'm prepared this time. He was cordial last we met. It will be fine."

Mindy gave Ken a hard look. "Do something."

He held up his hands. "I've already stuck my nose way too far into this. She's an adult and can make her own decisions."

"Mindy, don't put the poor man in the middle of this. I'll be careful. I promise."

Mindy nodded her resignation.

Dr. Drake had seemed truly sorry for his behavior, but his actions tomorrow would be telling.

Chapter Fifteen

Once Mar walked into her house, the answering machine's blinking red beacon pulled her toward it in a beeline.

Two messages.

The first one asked her to contact the nursing home Mrs. Thomas had been in. Mar returned the call. However, the afternoon duty nurse didn't know of any message from the morning and asked her to try again the following morning when the charge nurse could probably help her. Sighing, Mar hung up. "I wonder what anyone from there wanted with me. I've felt pretty much like *persona non grata* around there. I guess I'll find out tomorrow."

The second message was from the elusive Rose Swanson who said she and Paul had returned early, and she was eager to see Mar. Leaving a number, she said to call, even if it was late. "What's going on all of a sudden? Everything we've searched for so hard is turning up at once."

"You've worked tirelessly for all this information." Mindy squeezed Mar's shoulder. "I'm glad it's all coming together for you, and that I can be here to witness it."

"Me too. It's just strange to have gotten almost all the answers we need in a twenty-four-hour period. I'm going to call Rose. Don't forget that Diane is coming over later."

Mar dialed the number, and it was answered almost immediately by a soft, sweet voice very much as her mother's had been. Mar hoped Rose was as nice as she sounded. "I came across some things that raised questions about my mother and my birth. I would like to discuss them with someone who had been close to my mom back when she was pregnant with me and..."

"I'm anxious to see you and talk about anything you want. I'm sorry for not talking to you at Beth's funeral. You were surrounded by friends, so we decided it wasn't the right time to intrude. Right now, I'm headed out the door on an important errand. Can we meet in person? Perhaps tomorrow or the day after?"

"I would love to see you. I have a lunch meeting tomorrow. How about the afternoon?" Mar didn't want anything to get in the way of her lunch with Kevin. Only for the purpose of gaining her mom's medical records. That's what she told herself anyway.

"Afternoon's not good for me. How about early on Thursday?"

The day after tomorrow.

"Sounds good."

"Do you want to meet somewhere or I could come to your house?"

"If you don't mind coming to my place, that would be great." Mar felt comfortable inviting her over since she was a close friend of her mom's. "Let me give you the address."

"If it's the same house you grew up in, then I know how to get there with my eyes closed."

"Please don't drive blind." Mar chuckled as did Rose. When Mar hung up, the sense that a loving new presence had entered her life lingered with her.

Before Mar could even sit down, the phone rang. She answered and opted for a semi-professional voice. "Margaret Ross, how may I help you?"

"Mar, it's Dr. Kevin Drake. I'm at Orchard Park Nursing Home, and Mrs. Thomas has just passed away. I wouldn't have bothered you, but one of the nurses put on her chart that she had been urging them to contact you. It seems they tried several times today but couldn't get you. Do you have any idea what she wanted?"

Mar had been out most of the day. "Mrs. Thomas? No. I just got home. There was a message on my machine, but the duty nurse didn't know anything about why they were trying to reach me. So, it was Mrs. Thomas who had a message for me. I have no idea what it could be." She had hoped to visit the old woman tomorrow to get answers, but any she had, now had been taken to the grave.

"Since she was trying to get ahold of you, would you mind coming here? I realize it's last minute, but I need to be here for quite a while yet, filling out papers and waiting for the medical examiner. If you'll join me, we can go through her things."

"You're sorting her things? Why not a family member or the staff there?"

"Her nearest family is out of state, and they are understaffed here at the moment. I offered to help out. She may have left something for you, and I would appreciate the help."

Mar held the phone out in front of her face, looking at it unbelievingly for a second or two. This got stranger and stranger. "Certainly, Dr. Drake, I'd love to join you. If you're sure it's all right."

"Positive."

"Then I'll be there as quick as I can."

"Thanks, and call me Kevin. I'll see you soon." He hung up.

Mindy frowned. "Who was that?"

"Kev—Dr. Drake. We won't be getting any answers from Mrs. Thomas."

"What?" Mindy scowled now. "I thought after your new lunch date scheduled, he would let you visit her—even if it was supervised. Did he cancel lunch too?"

"No, that's not it at all. Mrs. Thomas passed away. The poor woman."

"Well, now I feel bad for my insensitive comments."

"You didn't know." Mar swung on her coat. "He wants me to help pack up her belongings."

"Or maybe he just wants to see you."

Mar liked that thought but chose not to comment on it. "I'll try to be back by the time Diane gets here." She headed out the door.

A short time later, she walked into the entrance of the nursing home. She asked at the nurse's station for Dr. Drake and was directed to Mrs. Thomas's room. She traversed the hallways. Strange how she and Kevin kept meeting under unusual circumstances and places they frequented yet never ran into each other before.

Kevin Drake was kneeling by the empty bed which had been stripped of its bedding. Mar was relieved Mrs. Thomas had been taken away already. Kevin appeared to be reaching for something underneath.

"Good afternoon, doctor."

He turned his head to see her. "Well, this is embarrassing." He stood, holding up a wood-carved pen. Expensive. "A graduation gift from my grandfather. Where are my manners? Good afternoon, Mar."

"Don't be embarrassed. I drop things all the time." She wanted to steer the conversation to why she was here. "I'm sorry to hear about Mrs. Thomas, especially since a friend and I were planning to visit her—with your permission, of course. I would have come sooner, but you were adamant."

"I hope we aren't going to start sparring. I truly am sorry about my actions. Shall we get on with the task at hand?"

"Exactly what is the task?" Mar glanced about the space.

"Clearing out her room of any personal items to make way for the next resident. I am really out of my element here." He opened the nightstand.

Mar did a quick assessment—nightstand, small dresser, and compact closet. "We'll need at least two boxes. I'll go check at the nurses' station." She headed for the lobby, procured three boxes, and returned.

Kevin stood by the dresser with a thoughtful expression. He held a manila envelope.

What was so enthralling? "That must be important."

"I haven't the faintest idea." He held it out to her. "This might be why the nursing home was trying to get a hold of you."

Looking closer, but still not taking it, she scrunched her eyebrows together. "That's me, Margaret Ross. I honestly didn't think she really knew my name."

"It's obviously for you."

What could Mrs. Thomas have left for her? She didn't want to open it in front of a relative stranger. She took the package, gingerly laying it on a chair with her bag and jacket. Turning back, Kevin held an identical envelope.

"Don't tell me that has my name on it too."

"No. Though it looks like more of the same. This one has a different name on it."

Leaning nearer to read the name, her breath caught—*Marilyn Gordon.*

"Do you know her?"

What should she tell him? What *could* she tell him? "We-ell," she began slowly, drawing out the word. "I don't know her—yet, but I do know she's the daughter of Dr. and Mrs. Thomas' niece. I'm planning to meet her very soon, if things work out. She's away right now, working overseas for an airline." Or something like that. "I met her best friend, Diane, earlier today, and she's coming over to my place later. We were planning to visit Mrs. Thomas together tomorrow, but now that's overcome by events."

Kevin's confused expression let Mar know she was doing it again, talking nonsense beyond his comprehension because he knew nothing of her dilemma. "I can't explain it. I don't know the whole story yet myself. It's part of why I was trying to get my mom's medical records." With tears brimming in her eyes, she turned to run away.

He spoke in a pleading, urgent voice. "Please don't go."

She halted but didn't face him.

"Mar, I haven't a clue here, but it's obviously very important. There seems to be some sort of a mystery in all this. Let's go somewhere that we can talk."

"What about the rest of her stuff? I thought we were going to sort it out."

"We can stay here, but let's sit." He guided her over to the chair, then sat on the edge of the bed. "Shall we start with your mother's death?"

Mar shook her head. "Dr. Thomas wasn't her doctor at that time, but he was her doctor when she was pregnant with me." And my twin. "I need her medical records because of something *medical-related* I learned from her old diaries."

"Patty assumed Dr. Thomas might be accused of something illegal. We in the medical community can be very protective of our own. Now that both Dr. and Mrs. Thomas are deceased, it shouldn't matter anymore. What exactly are you looking for?"

What, indeed. That her whole life had been a lie? That the Thomases had robbed her of her sister? The smallest notation in the records could be further proof—one way or another. The twin envelope addressed to Marilyn was a huge indicator.

Mindy had cautioned her against insisting on having her mom's records before he knew her for himself, but the can was open and worms were everywhere. "I never wanted to hurt the Thomases." She unraveled the story for him as coherently as possible, beginning with the discovery in her mom's room and then leading on to the Gordons and their daughter, Marilyn.

"This has to be so hard for you. Now that you know who she is and where to find her, what are you going to do?"

She explained who Ken was and the potential decision to let him go to Arizona to talk to Marilyn's parents before she took any other steps. "Of course, it's terribly hard to wait now that I am able to find her. I don't think she's ever had any indication she isn't their own child. We figured it would be better to let her parents tell her."

"Is that why you're not terribly eager to open your package from Mrs. Thomas?"

"I guess so." She shrugged. "I feel it might be a letdown after searching so hard for the answers, and she had them all the time. I'll wait 'til I feel up to it, and I'm alone to delve into whatever's in that envelope."

"Do you feel better now? Shall we finish what we started here?" He made a sweeping gesture with his hand.

"Definitely." She expected Diane at her house soon so had limited time. "I'll sort out clothes for the women's shelter but let Ruth Gordon decide if that's what she wants to do with them. We can put personal items in another box for her as well. It will save her a bit of the burden of it all."

A nurse stopped by the room. "How's it going in here?"

"Good. I'm glad I have Miss Ross to help me."

"We really appreciate you doing this so we don't have to. We'll put the boxes in storage until her niece can come for them or tell us what she wants to be done with them." The nurse lifted her chin slightly. "Speaking of which, we have informed Ruth Gordon, and she and her husband are taking the next flight up here."

Mar was glad to know that. So, Ken wouldn't have to go to Arizona to speak to them.

"Excellent. I don't know if you were the nurse who spoke to Miss Ross or not about Mrs. Thomas wanting to see her. But she had an envelope for her, so I gave it to her."

"Thanks." She shifted her attention to down the hall where a beeping sound came from. "Duty calls." She left.

Kevin emptied a dresser drawer, sorting the clothes into piles ready to put into boxes.

Mar pointed to the closet. "Shall I tackle this?" When Kevin agreed, she opened the door to it. Not a whole lot in here. She removed a couple of hanging dresses and something puffy encased in a plastic garment bag. After carrying them over to the bed, she unzipped the garment bag several inches to reveal a fur coat. "I'm amazed someone didn't take this."

"That is surprising."

Back at the closet, she retrieved the two pairs of shoes from the bottom. "Did you come across Mrs. Thomas's purse among the rest of her stuff?"

"No, but I can check for it on the shelf." Kevin walked over and reached up to the closet shelf. "I don't know how they expect old people to use these. This is almost too high for me." He gave her the bag, then swiped his hand along the shelf again and retrieved two old-fashioned photo albums. "I'll bet someone put these here when she moved in, and she never saw them since."

Mar took the albums and sat in the chair. "Do you think it would be all right if I peek at these?"

"Sure. Go for it. A perk of cleaning out someone else's belongings."

Mar opened the first one and flipped quickly then stopped dead. Her breath caught as her face looked back at her from a baby picture. Then her life unfolded before her as Marilyn grew up. Not her life, but her twin's. Somehow, she knew how Marilyn was likely feeling in each photo. Mar had similar photos of herself as a baby, the first day of school, prom. She had missed so much. Her vision blurred.

Kevin knelt in front of her. "Are you all right?"

She pointed to several photos of Marilyn as a teenager, tapping the prom picture. "That's almost the same dress I wore to prom, and our dates could be brothers." It was freaky, but kind of cool at the same time.

Kevin's expression turned incredulous. "It's amazing how much she resembles you." He captured her gaze with his. "If I didn't believe you are deadly serious about all this, I would never guess these were pictures of anyone but you. I understand how people could mistake you for her."

With her palms, she wiped the tears from her cheeks. "We are identical. Except for being raised by different parents." She tapped a graduation photo. "This is her friend Diane standing next to her. I just met her today. In fact, I'm supposed to be meeting her at my house."

"You go on. I'll finish up here and let the staff know we're done. They'll put her belongings in storage until her niece can claim them."

"What about the envelope for Marilyn Gordon?"

"I'll take it and let the staff here know I have it."

"Thanks. Bye." Mar gathered up her coat, purse, and the large manila envelope that hopefully contained the secrets of her past. Perhaps, how she and Marilyn got separated.

"Until lunch tomorrow."

Smiling, she nodded as she exited. Then she hurried home in the waning light in hopes of arriving before Diane. As she pulled into her driveway, Diane stepped out of her car parked in front. Mar climbed from her BMW.

Diane met her there. "Perfect timing." She shook her head. "I almost called you Marilyn. I don't know if I'll ever get used to there being two of you—or her."

"It is strange, but I look forward to getting used to this order of things." Mar hesitated a moment. "I have bad news. Mrs. Thomas passed away today."

"Oh, no. And we were going to go see her tomorrow."

Mar chose not to mention that the large envelope in her arms was from the recently departed. "Come on in. I want you to meet Ken and Mindy." Diane followed her inside.

The couple sat on the couch but stood when they saw Diane.

Mar made the introductions.

Mindy edged closer to Mar. "Is she really so very much like Marilyn that they could easily be mistaken for each other?"

"That's for sure." Diane nodded heartily. "I really thought Marilyn had returned until Mar convinced me she was an entirely different person. Even now, I need to remind myself she isn't Marilyn." She dug into her canvas shoulder bag. "I brought school pictures, some of her in her airline uniform, and a bunch of various snapshots so you can see for yourselves." She produced a large envelope full of pictures.

Mar sat on the sofa with Diane who handed her photos. Mar then passed them on to Mindy and Ken in flanking chairs. All comments were about how identical the girl in the pictures was to Mar.

After the photos made the rounds, Diane received the stack back from Ken. "Okay, Mar, it's your turn for show and tell. Let's see what set you off on this sister hunt in the first place."

"Of course." Mar waved to the piles on the coffee table, but she didn't include the Thomas envelope she hadn't ventured to peruse yet. It could say something bad about her parents. Could they have willingly given Marilyn away? Didn't want to know that. Couldn't imagine it. Or it could be a bunch of nothing. As long as she didn't open it, there was still hope. "It all started with this." She plucked one of the diaries from the table and handed it to Diane. "Page twenty-seven near the bottom." She had the book practically memorized.

Mindy snatched the letters and handed them to Diane. "I think she should start with your parents' correspondence."

Ken pulled out the legal documents. "The birth and marriage certificates are the ones that hold irrefutable facts." They were added to Diane's growing pile.

Laughing, Diane threw up her hands. "Whoa, let's do one thing at a time." She pulled the diary from the bottom of the pile on her lap. "It started with this, right?"

"Well, it's like this. I was going through Mom's dresser and closet to find things to donate to the women's shelter." Mar related the chain of events, including her recent trip to the nursing home, but still excluded the Thomas envelope. She actually did want to dive into it whether it had answers or not, but also wanted to soak up every bit of information Diane had to impart.

Diane tapped her lips with her index finger. "So, you deduced there had been two babies, but how did you figure out Marilyn was the other one?"

"It took hard work from all three of us, but we finally discovered Mrs. Gordon was Dr. Thomas' niece from the funeral home. She had taken care of all the finances. Then last night when we were out, an old neighbor recognized me as Marilyn. That put us on the track to Tacoma where we knew the Gordons had lived. That's how I found you because the neighbor was Carolyn's grandmother, Mrs. Iverson."

"I've met her several times. If she didn't think you were Marilyn, she would have called you out on it. Of that, you can be sure."

"I can't stand it any longer." Mar jumped to her feet and retrieved the Thomas envelope from the kitchen where she'd stashed it when she'd come in with Diane. "I wanted to wait and go through this in private, but it might contain vital information. Or it might have nothing useful at all." She was sure her mom never would have given Marilyn away willingly, so there was nothing to fear.

Mindy crinkled her eyebrows. "What is it?"

Mar took a deep breath, knowing she could still back out. "Mrs. Thomas left this for me. I think that was why the nursing home had left me a message."

"What's in it? What does it say?"

"I don't know."

Mindy's eyes widened like beach balls. "How could you have something like that and not tear into it? Don't you want answers?"

"I was afraid it might not have any answers."

"You're right." Mindy stood and crossed to Mar, hooking her arm around Mar's shoulders. "It may tell you nothing. But if you don't open it, you definitely won't get any answers."

Mindy's support meant the world to Mar. "And you're right too." Drawing in a long slow breath, she turned the envelope over and bent up the metal tabs.

Here went nothing.

Chapter Sixteen

Three pairs of eyes gazed expectantly at Mar, urging her to reveal the secrets the envelope held. She glanced at her friends. "Maybe I should read this alone first."

Mindy squeezed Mar's shoulders with the arm that was around her. "This is your family, your information, your puzzle to piece together. We will all be here for you, no matter what you choose to do." She ushered her back to the couch. "Why don't you sit down again?"

Mar obeyed.

"Now, do you want us to leave you? We can go into the kitchen. Or may we stay to support you?"

Looking at each of her friends, she drank in their love and compassion. "You can stay, but I'm going to read to myself first if you don't mind."

Mindy immediately reseated herself before Mar finished her sentence. "We will remain as quiet as church mice while you read."

As Mar freed the flap from the metal prongs, her insides spiraled about like a tornado. "I almost forgot. She left an identical envelope for Marilyn Gordon. That is one more validation that she is indeed my twin and the Thomases' involvement."

Mindy gave a firm nod. "I'll say."

Diane tilted her head. "One glimpse of you and there's no question about it."

This was easier for Diane to believe because she had actual knowledge of Marilyn and what she looked like. Mar only had other people's word for it—and a few photos. She studied her name on the envelope, slipped her hand inside, and pulled out a stack of papers. On the top sat a business-sized envelope with Elizabeth Ross written on it. "This is addressed to my mother. I'll wait to open that." She set it aside. The next paper appeared to be a letter.

> *Dear Margaret Ross,*
>
> *I have lived with what we did for all these years. I replay the events in my mind over and over and ask myself if I would have done anything differently. There's no other way to put it than we stole one life to save another. I don't know what else we could have done.*

The letter went on to tell the tragic story of Ruth Gordon, a decade or more older than Mar's mom, struggling to have a child. Each of her pregnancies either never made it full term or ended in a stillbirth. With her husband away at war, she teetered on the edge of her breaking point. They had prayed for Ruth's baby to be healthy and thrive. Her sanity depended on it.

She described how Ruth went into labor which had been rough and long. The baby didn't survive, a little girl with peach-fuzz hair.

How sad. There had been another little baby who hadn't made it. Mar allowed herself a moment of grief for the loss. She viewed the real Gordon baby, born the same day, as a sister, too, in light of all the events that had taken place. Triplets.

> *We didn't know how we were going to tell her she'd lost yet another child.*
>
> *Then we received the call that your mother was in labor. Leaving Ruth sedated and sleeping, we rushed to Beth's. She hadn't been sleeping well and was exhausted, but her labor was*

easy in comparison. Though born a month early, both babies seemed healthy and strong.

In a moment of weakness, I rushed out of the room with the second infant, before your mother saw her.

Mar had wondered who was older, her or Marilyn. Mar was the "big" sister. Cool. She continued reading.

She was so perfect. Why couldn't Ruth's have been perfect? Ruth was my sister's only child and my only family. I couldn't lose her. A few minutes later, Edgar came out and asked what was wrong. I showed him the baby's face and told him that she could be Ruth's baby. Eventually, he reluctantly agreed and told your mother the "other" infant didn't make it. A half-truth, because of Ruth's little one. Though sad, your mother seemed happy to have a healthy daughter. It worked, and Ruth thrived being a mother.

I fantasized many times about having the two of you accidentally meet, but then what we had done would come out and couldn't be kept quiet. Once you travel down an unspeakable path, as we did, it's best to never bring it up. Pretend nothing untoward happened.

Is what we did wrong? No one was physically harmed by our actions. We saved Ruth's sanity, and the baby was loved and well cared for. She had everything she could have ever wanted. Your mother would have struggled caring for two newborns alone with your father away. It was really best for everyone. Or so we told ourselves to ease our consciences. Too late to erase the past.

Forgive us and find your sister. Her name is Marilyn Gordon.

Helen Thomas

Mar read the letter again to make sure she had understood correctly.

It was as they had suspected. The Thomases had given Mar's twin to someone else. Someone who had suffered great losses. Mar held the paper to one side so she could see the next one.

Mindy softly cleared her throat. "May I?"

Absentmindedly, Mar handed it over as she perused a medical paper.

Diane rose from the couch and moved around behind Mindy's chair. Ken, too, got up to read over Mindy's shoulder.

Several medical papers with notes about the delivery of the twins as well as a photocopy of an alternate birth certificate for the Gordons's child. One with no name. A document from the West Seattle Cemetery where the deceased baby had been laid to rest. The same one that Dr. Thomas was buried at, and soon Mrs. Thomas. "Hey, Mindy. Wasn't there an infant grave near Dr. Thomas's? A "Baby G"?

Mindy lifted her tear-rimmed gaze. "I don't remember." She slightly raised the letter to Mar. "This is unbelievable. Even though this is what we suspected."

Mar nodded, not ready to discuss it yet. She was sure there had been that grave as well as a marker for Mrs. Thomas with a birth date but not one for death. December 29, 1998, would soon be added. Mar had assumed the "G" in "Baby G" stood for an unnamed "girl", but it more likely stood for Baby Gordon. They must not have wanted to spell out the name for fear Ruth might see and question it.

She continued through the stack, handing each new sheet to Mindy. At the bottom was an envelope labeled "photos".

Taking a deep breath, she pulled out the stack. Photos of herself. Or were they Marilyn? A few she recognized as her early school pictures. She had identicals in her own photo albums. Mom must have given those to them. A lot of doctors received periodic photos of children they had delivered. The back of each one was carefully labeled with either Margaret or Marilyn. So surreal to see someone who looked exactly like herself.

Lastly, she opened the envelope addressed to her mom. It held two letters. In the first, dated the year after Mar was born, Mrs. Thomas explained how the separation occurred and begged for forgiveness. In the second, dated last year after Beth's death, she said she had meant to mail the first letter several times over the years, that there was nothing that could be done now about the events that had taken place so long ago. Mrs. Thomas had eaten herself up inside. "I'll go to my grave knowing what I have done and you never knowing your other daughter."

Mar blinked back tears and sat perfectly still.

Once everyone had read all the papers and studied the photos, the room fell silent for several minutes. Mar turned her head from side to side in disbelief. "Do you guys understand the implication of all this?"

Ken spoke in a matter-of-fact manner. "An indisputable crime was committed."

Mindy frowned. "It's terrible. What are you going to do, Mar?"

"I thought I knew, but now I don't."

Diane thinned her lips. "I don't see how this changes anything for you or Marilyn. Didn't you say Mrs. Thomas left a similar envelope for her?"

"Oh, no. Maybe I can talk Dr. Drake into not giving it to her."

"You will do no such thing." Diane straightened. "I'm not sure how each of the Gordons will take the news, but I don't see how you can even think of not informing them either morally or legally. They have the right to make their own decisions on how to handle this situation."

Openmouthed, Mar regarded Diane, unable to believe what she'd heard. "I don't understand your total lack of concern for the Gordons as a family. How do you think this will affect them?"

Diane didn't flinch or back down. "It's not up to you to protect the others. How would you feel if the roles were reversed? I doubt you would appreciate this being kept from you. If you do decide not to tell Marilyn *and* convince Dr. Drake to not give them the package, at some point in the future the truth *will* come out. And Marilyn would feel cheated out of whatever years passed from now until then."

Mar knew Diane was right. "This is all too incredible to believe. How could Ruth or her husband not know the baby they were presented with wasn't theirs?"

Diane gave a sympathetic look. "I'm sorry to say that it's actually pretty easy. Doctors are authority figures. People naturally accept whatever a doctor tells them."

Mar had to admit that she did.

Ken hunched his shoulders in an almost shrug. "At least we know that the perpetrated act wasn't a premeditated crime, though still illegal."

"So, what should I do? I was sure the Gordons knew Marilyn wasn't their biological child, having adopted her, and therefore half the battle was already taken care of. But how do you convince people that something they've known as the truth for nearly thirty years is a lie? This all got a whole lot harder. Will this news cause Mrs. Gordon to have the breakdown the Thomases feared? That could drive a wedge between them and me. Marilyn might never accept me as a sister. They may refuse to accept the facts and close ranks with me on the outside. I had imagined a happy reunion, not horrible facts forced down their throats. Should I give this up and wait for them to come to me?"

"No!" Mindy, Ken, and Diane all spoke emphatically at the same time.

Diane's expression became stern. "Don't even think that way. Your mom and Mrs. Thomas set these wheels in motion when they left evidence for you."

Ken spoke. "And the information package Mrs. Thomas left for each twin takes this decision out of your hands. It's not your place to play God, the Thomases did that long ago."

Mar froze for a few moments. "I guess I feel as though the Gordons should be left as a family since they've never known they really weren't."

Mindy's expression held compassion. "They shouldn't be any more hurt or shocked by this information than you've been. At least they still have each other, and while this will surely rock their comfortable world, you need to remember you're not the cause of this problem, you're one of the victims. All the principals are deceased now and can't be charged with a crime."

"I know Marilyn." Diane nodded. "Even if it's hard to accept or deal with, she would want to know. So, you—we *will* tell her. The question is how and when with the least hurt feelings and damage."

Mindy sat up straighter. "What about a DNA test to assuage any doubts?"

Ken's face turned sober. "Though indisputable, it could hamper Marilyn's acceptance of her. Going to court and forcing them to see the truth might cause a permanent rift."

Mar's insides tightened. "I don't want to go to court. That could hurt Marilyn and her family. I know what it's like to lose your parents. I don't want Marilyn to lose hers over this."

Ken raised his eyebrows. "Technically, they aren't her parents."

Mindy shot Ken a murderous look, and he shrunk at the wordless scolding. Then she turned a bright smile on Mar. "You always were selfless and thoughtful. Everyone else comes first with you."

Mar appreciated her friend sticking up for her. "The Gordons raised Marilyn. They *are* her parents. Besides John Gordon isn't in good health. What might a shock like this do to him? If, after receiving the information from Mrs. Thomas, they don't want to see me, I'll respect that."

Diane returned to the couch. "As I said, Marilyn is definitely going to want to meet you."

Mar ached for that to be true. "Even if her parents don't want her to? Even if it kills her father?"

"She's an adult who can make her own decisions. You are not responsible for Mr. Gordon. He will be fine."

Mar could hear the unspoken *hopefully* in Diane's confidence.

Ken cringed as though afraid to speak after the silent reprimand he'd received previously. "The Gordons will arrive in the morning. Let's see if Dr. Drake is amenable to arranging a meeting with Ruth Gordon so we can present the evidence to her. Perhaps, he can learn John Gordon's physical condition. This will all come out eventually. Better sooner than later."

Mar agreed. "It sounds like we have a plan." She prayed it would all go smoothly.

Chapter Seventeen

Glancing down at her watch, Mar was startled at the time. "It's nearly seven-thirty." She and the others had been so wrapped up in the envelope's puzzling contents that the time had flown. "I'm starved. Anyone else hungry? We can order pizza or something. Diane, you're welcome to stay."

Ken stood. "I can whip up chicken alfredo. I brought all the ingredients. There will be plenty for you too, Diane."

"Sounds delicious. I need to eat anyway, but I'll have to leave right after. I have to be at work by six in the morning."

Soon enough Mar sat at the kitchen table with her three friends. After stuffing themselves, Diane thanked everyone and promised to return tomorrow.

Mar forced a yawn. "I know it's barely nine, but I'm exhausted. I'm heading to bed." Wanting to give the lovebirds some time alone, she offered a limp wave and ambled down the hall.

When the phone rang, she hustled into her room and picked up the extension.

A business-like voice came through the line. "Miss Margaret Ross, please."

When she identified herself, the woman continued. "Miss Ross, this is nurse Jordan at Harborview Hospital. Dr. Drake asked me to call and requests that you come as soon as possible. There has been an accident. I have no details. He's busy with the patient and couldn't call himself. Are you available?"

"Of course, I'm on my way. Can you give me any more information?"

"No, I'm sorry. He wants you at the emergency entrance right away."

She hung up and hurried to the back door for her coat. Swinging it on, she called out to Ken and Mindy. "I'm needed at the hospital."

Mindy appeared in the kitchen. "Is it serious?"

Mar shrugged. "They didn't tell me anything. It's the hospital ER, so it could be anything from mildly urgent to deadly serious." But if Kevin was requesting her presence, she would lean toward the graver end of things. "Don't wait up."

"We'll pray for you and whoever is in need."

"Thanks." Mar rushed to her car. Her mind whirled during the fifteen-minute drive. What kind of an accident could it be? Was it someone she knew and loved, or someone who would need help getting home or to the shelter after treatment? Once parked in the emergency area, she ran through the open doors. Glancing about for someone to tell her what was up, she stopped at the sight of Betsy Littlefoot and her children looking helpless, huddled near a treatment room.

Going to them, she threw her arms around the whole group. "Betsy, what's happened? I got a call. Did you ask for me?"

Sobbing, the woman hugged Mar tightly. "Dr. Drake must have called you before we got here. Bless him. He's so good to us all."

"Yes, but what's the problem? Is it your mom?"

"No." Betsy gasped in a shuddered breath. "It's Johnny. He was driving a logging truck up on the Olympic Peninsula and went off the road, coming down that terrible area by the Quinault on Highway 101. It was several hours before they found him. Thank God he didn't go into the lake. We would have lost him for sure."

Mar sent up a silent prayer for the man.

Betsy continued. "Then they brought him here by helicopter, and Dr. Drake called me. He doesn't know if Johnny can pull through or not. I'm so glad you're here with me, Mar. I just don't know what to do."

At that moment, the curtains opened, and two aides pushed Johnny's stretcher with various hanging bags of fluid. Kevin trailed close on their heels. "Heading upstairs to the operating room. The specialists are scrubbing for surgery."

"Come on, guys." Mar bent down to the children who looked bewildered. "Let's go up to a better waiting room, and I'll get you some snacks." She took the two youngest by the hands and followed after the disappearing gurney with Betsy hurrying along behind, holding onto her eldest's hand.

After taking a few minutes to get the children settled around a waiting room table, Mar led Betsy over to a pair of chairs in a corner. "Take a few deep breaths and fill me in. We'll let the medical staff focus on their jobs. They'll do their very best."

"I know, Mar, but it's so hard to just wait and not be able to help. Especially when it's someone you love. I can't stand to think this might be the end of our family."

"Tell me everything Dr. Drake and anyone else has told you."

"I only saw him for a minute when I got here. Right after he saw Johnny. He's concerned there's internal damage, you know, bleeding inside. He has a broken leg, a dislocated shoulder, and a concussion. I think that last one worries them most. There could be other things they don't know about yet. How can he possibly get well with all those things wrong? I'm so scared he'll never be my Johnny again. What will the kids do? He's the best father in the world to them." At that, she broke into even louder sobs.

Mar put her arms around the distraught woman. Mar's troubles were minuscule compared to Betsy's. "Try to calm down for your children's sake. They need you to be strong." It couldn't be good for the kids to see their mother so upset. Mar had never seen the woman so panic-stricken, even when she was the one hurt.

Betsy looked up through her tears. "I'll try. I'm just so terribly afraid for him." She had reason to be fearful. Johnny's injuries could be severe.

Mar motioned toward the door. "Well, no one's come through there to tell us he's gone. That's a point for the good. Tell me about what happened."

Sucking in a couple of deep breaths, Betsy related what she knew. "The logging company he was hauling for is up out of Forks. He took the job so far away because the pay was good, and it was only supposed to last a couple of months. It was around seven when I got a call from the Clallam County Sheriff's Department." She lowered her voice, presumably to keep the children from hearing the gory details. "They said Johnny had been in an accident and airlifted to Seattle. Johnny was hauling on Highway 101 into a log yard in Grays Harbor. That's a really nasty stretch of road going down the grade along Lake Quinault. Johnny had a full load, and on one of those narrow curves, he must have lost control. They reckon he was down in the brush and trees for some time before he was missed."

Mar's insides twisted at the thought of being all alone and injured.

Betsy drew in a labored, deep breath. "Finally, one of the truckers asked if he'd been in to unload. When they said he hadn't arrived at the scales, the other driver called back to the company who phoned the sheriff. They sent search and rescue along the road. It was a little while before the wreck was spotted."

Mar listened carefully to the details.

"It took over an hour to get him out of the truck and into Forks where a helicopter airlifted him here. He must have been in the wreck for at least four hours. I hate to think of him suffering so long not knowing if someone would find him." Betsy's gaze flickered to the door. "You're right, as usual though. They're still in there, so he must still be alive. I wanted to call you and probably should have but decided to wait."

Mar was grateful Kevin had the hospital contact her. "How did you find out so many details about the accident?"

"Right after I got here, the owner of the company Johnny was hauling for called. He wanted to know if the helicopter had landed yet, but they hadn't, so I had time to hear everything."

Mar glanced at the children sitting listlessly at the table. "I thought your mom had your kids."

"She dropped them off before noon and headed over to Spokane with her sister. I haven't been able to get a hold of her yet."

"We'll try her again later."

The youngest Littlefoot child slunk over and climbed up onto Betsy's lap and snuggled in with eyes closed. The little mite would be asleep before long. The other two had laid their heads on their arms on the table, almost asleep as well.

Mar patted Betsy's arm. "Let me see if I can wrestle up some pillows and blankets." She headed for the nurse's station and returned with her desired bounty. She settled the two older children on a pair of couches in the room and covered them. Then she left again, returning with two Styrofoam cups of hot chocolate from the machine in the hall and handed one to Betsy. "No news is good news."

Betsy hugged her child closer and nodded.

Mar ached for this frightened mother. "Some of Johnny's injuries sound pretty serious."

"Do you know anything about head injuries? I've heard all kinds of horror stories, and I don't know what to believe."

Head traumas were tricky. "From what I understand, some people wake up just like they were before, while others have difficulties for a year or two because usually both the short-term memory and the emotional control area are damaged." And still, others never regained their mental functions, but no sense scaring her with that unnecessarily.

"We won't know for some time how Johnny's head will be, but we'll pray for the best."

The two women sat silently, sipping their cocoa and watching the sleeping children. After a bit, Betsy rose and put her baby on a third couch. She turned to Mar. "I'll try to get my mom again. They should be at their destination by now." She went to the tier of public phones and made the call. When she returned, she told Mar she'd talked to her mother and told her what had happened. She'd promised to call again as soon as she knew Johnny's condition. "I don't want her to worry any more than necessary or try to rush home in the middle of the night. It's a five-hour drive and that's if the passes are good, without snow and ice."

"Wise decision. She wouldn't be able to do much, but I'm sure she would be a comfort to you and the kids." Mar indicated the chair. "Why don't you sit back down?"

Shaking her head, Betsy wrung her hands. "I'm too jittery to sit." She paced the waiting room. "What can be taking them so long? They've been in there for hours." She flopped back into a chair and put her head in her hands and moaned.

Every minute must seem like an eternity. It had felt like that for Mar sitting next to her ill mother, waiting for either a miracle or death to ease her pain. Mar rubbed the distraught woman's back to comfort her.

After another hour, the doors leading toward the operating room burst open, and Kevin strode through them, unfastening his mask. He wore a tired smile.

Mar and Betsy stood. Mar put her arm around the young mother.

Stretching his muscles, Kevin walked toward them. "We patched Johnny up, and he's holding his own at this point. We'll be moving him down to recovery in a little while, and then he'll go to the critical care unit. After we get him moved, you can have a few minutes. I'm sure Mar will watch the kids while you do that. It's going to be a long, rough haul until he's the old Johnny again, but I think that will happen. It'll just take time."

Betsy gave a shaky nod. "So all that bleeding inside him wasn't too much?"

Kevin thinned his lips. "I won't lie. He's pretty banged up. Dr. Waters repaired some minor internal bleeding and relieved pressure on his brain. Time will tell how bad it is. Dr. Ingstrom, the orthopedist, reset his dislocated shoulder but will need to wait until the swelling goes down in his leg before casting the broken bone."

Mar resisted the urge to gasp. Johnny Littlefoot was fortunate to be alive.

Kevin continued. "It'll take time for his head to repair itself. The other two doctors will speak to you soon and explain things better. Good news is, your Johnny has an iron will to live. I'll change my gown and walk you to recovery."

Kevin returned shortly in a clean scrub suit and walked up to Mar. "I hope I did the right thing by calling you. I knew Betsy would need someone she knew and trusted no matter which way things went. Thanks for coming without asking questions."

"Oh, I had plenty of questions. Still do, but they can wait. Now, take Betsy to see her husband."

He turned to the young mother who had gone over to kiss each of her children. "You ready, Mrs. Littlefoot?"

She nodded, and the pair headed down the corridor.

Mar envied Betsy a little. Though the situation was horrific, at least she had a hopeful prognosis.

Not more than fifteen minutes later, Kevin Drake and Betsy returned. Betsy held her head a little higher than when she left.

Kevin addressed Mar. "I told Mrs. Littlefoot—"

"Doctor?" Betsy warned.

"Pardon me. I told *Betsy*, I want her and the kids to go home and get some rest. The staff here will take good care of her husband and will call her the minute he wakes. Can you help her get the children to her car?"

"Of course." Mar didn't need to be asked.

"Thank you."

Betsy crossed to her children and roused them.

Kevin touched Mar's arm. "Before you go, I wanted to ask if you opened the envelope from Mrs. Thomas."

"I did."

"Was it good news? I don't mean to pry."

"Not exactly. I can return once Betsy and the kids are off, if you have time?"

"Sure. I'll confer with Mr. Littlefoot's other doctors and meet you in the waiting room."

"Perfect." Mar would appreciate a doctor's point of view on the secrets revealed in the envelope. She helped to get the sleepy children up and out to Betsy's car.

Betsy gripped Mar's hand before closing the driver's door. "Thank you so much for everything."

"I'm happy to help. Call me if you need anything."

After the Littlefoots drove off, Mar headed back inside and was soon sitting in the waiting room with Kevin Drake. She conveyed the additional puzzle pieces the envelope held.

Kevin rubbed the stubble on his chin. "Would you mind making a copy of the contents?"

"Why? You have Marilyn's. I'm sure it holds identical information."

"Though I have possession of it, I can't open it without Marilyn Gordon's permission. But her par—Mr. and Mrs. Gordon will be arriving . . . Since it's way after midnight—they will arrive tomorrow, New Year's Eve. I have a meeting with the Gordons. I would like to present them with these developments."

"You would do that?"

"Sure. I would also like to present them with the most compelling evidence of all."

"What's that?"

"You."

Chapter Eighteen

Mar slept in again. She'd meant to set an alarm, but by the time she'd arrived home in the middle of the night, she'd evidently forgotten.

Since she was meeting Kevin Drake for lunch, she dressed in a maroon broomstick skirt and a pink blouse. A little bit dressy, a little bit feminine, but not over the top as though she was trying too hard—even though she had labored over her clothing choice for forty-five minutes. She must have auditioned ten different outfits, finally opting for what made her feel the most comfortable.

She headed to the kitchen where Mindy and Ken, once again, sat at her kitchen table like an old married couple. "Morning."

Mindy looked up from her section of the paper. "Morning. What was the emergency last night?"

"The Littlefoots. Except it was Johnny Littlefoot needing medical attention this time."

Mindy's eyes widened. "Did Betsy . . . ?"

Mar shook her head. "She would never. A trucking accident. Broken leg, dislocated shoulder, some minor internal bleeding they were able to stop, and a concussion. That's what has everyone the most worried. Kevin's not sure yet what the extent of the damage could be."

Mindy smirked. "Kevin?"

Mar smiled too. "Yes. He was there and assisted in the operating room. We talked afterward, and we still have our lunch date."

Grabbing a plate from the table, Ken held it up. "We have bagels and cream cheese for breakfast."

Mar snatched a bagel. "I don't have time to sit down. I need to make copies of the items Mrs. Thomas left me for Kevin. He wants to show them to the Gordons after they arrive tomorrow."

Mindy quirked an eyebrow. "He's going to help you?"

Mar widened her eyes. "I know. He seems to be as interested in getting to the bottom of this as we are." This confirmed that he *was* someone special. "I'll be back this afternoon." She clutched the bagel between her teeth as she swung on her coat and scooped up her purse and the envelope with an extra for the copies. With a wave to her friends, she headed out the door.

At the office supply store, Mar took her place in line at the counter. Between the string of people waiting, the machines malfunctioning, and an unruly customer, it took nearly an hour to have the copies made. Once back in her car, she jammed the copies into the spare large envelope. Oh dear, she would be over twenty minutes late.

At 11:52, she pulled into the parking lot with trepidation, remembering how things had ended the last time they'd tried to have lunch. She scanned the cars and spotted one she believed to be Kevin's. Good, he hadn't given up on her. When she entered the restaurant, he stood and waved her over to a table.

He didn't seem at all upset about her tardiness but instead smiled at her.

Her insides reacted with a little happy dance. "Sorry for being late. The copy place ended up being a huge hassle." She set her purse and envelope on the table.

"Not a problem." He assisted her off with her coat. "If I'm honest, I only arrived five minutes ago and hoped you hadn't already left." He pulled out a chair for her. Such a gentleman.

"Thanks." She sat and handed him the duplicate envelope. "Per your request."

"Thank you. I'll read these over so I'm prepared."

"You'll let me know when you're meeting with them, won't you?"

"Of course."

"So, why were you late?"

"I stopped in to check on John Littlefoot. He's doing as well as can be expected. Perhaps even a little better. Though not in a coma, he hasn't woken up yet. The longer he sleeps, the better off he'll be with the healing process. His blood pressure, temperature, and other vital signs are stable. I expect him to wake up later today or tomorrow. Mrs. Littlefoot was already there."

"Thank you for the update. Did she have the kids with her? Should I go get them so she can focus on Johnny?"

"Someone was looking after them, and her mom will arrive later today to help her out. Then Betsy can stay with her husband as much as she likes."

That was a relief. Mar would do whatever she could for the Littlefoots, but right now, she was grateful to be able to focus on her life-altering twin puzzle. So many pieces had fallen into place. With a few more, she would have a real sister in her life.

The waiter came over with waters, and they gave him their order.

"Did you tell your friends about me showing the Gordons copies of the Thomas envelope contents?"

"I did. They think it's a great idea. Having a doctor present them with the information will be much more credible than some random stranger, even if that stranger looks exactly like their daughter."

Kevin leaned forward. "Does it bother you to call her *their* daughter when you know she's not?"

"Oh, but she is. The Gordons raised her. I don't want to deprive her of them, I merely want to share her."

"What if they make things difficult? Or try to turn her against you?"

"I hope that doesn't happen. I've been praying and believe God will work it all out in His timing." She prayed His timing was soon.

The corner of his mouth quirked up at her mention of God. Another good sign.

"I've started the paperwork so you can obtain your mother's medical records legally. There shouldn't be any problems. I have a friend who might be able to expedite the process."

"I appreciate that." Though she didn't really need the records anymore with the Thomases' information and confession.

He patted the envelope. "Do you want to give me the rundown of what's in here? Or shall I be surprised?"

She gave him a quick summary of the contents and what the Thomases had done.

He shook his head. "It boggles my mind that anyone would do that, let alone a doctor. It goes against everything we stand for. What made you suspect something was amiss to start looking in the first place?"

She spilled her two-week quest as they ate, then they talked easily for some time about this and that.

He glanced at his watch. "I didn't realize it was so late. I need to run." He pulled out his wallet and handed his credit card over to the waiter before returning his attention to Mar. "Would you mind making a few more copies?"

"Of what?"

"The pertinent information in your mother's journals and correspondence between your parents. Not all of it, merely what you think matters."

"Sure. If it will help ease them into believing, then I'm all for it."

He escorted her out and opened her car door. "I'll call you to let you know when I'm meeting with the Gordons. You can bring the new copies then."

"I hope this works."

"Me too. I want to start by talking to Mrs. Gordon, and her husband if she thinks his health can take it. I want to present her with the facts—from her aunt no less—plus your other information. It should be enough to convince them. You said Diane was Marilyn's friend. Would she be willing to call the Gordons tonight to find out if Marilyn will be coming to whatever service they're having for Mrs. Thomas?"

Mar nodded. "Sure. Thank you for being so willing to help."

He smiled with a half-shrug. "I like . . . a good mystery." He closed her door and strode off.

Had he been going to say something else? Perhaps that he liked her? She liked that he liked a good mystery.

And she definitely liked him.

Chapter Nineteen

The next morning, Mar woke from pleasant dreams of a certain handsome doctor. She stretched her arms over her head and sighed. She wished she could go back to her sweet slumber, but she couldn't. The day ahead was busy and full of potential. Rose Swanson was due this morning and, later, the appointment with the Gordons. Her stomach twirled not only with giddy anticipation of the upcoming encounter with them—and eventually coming face-to-face with Marilyn—but also fear of being rejected by them all.

When she'd arrived home yesterday afternoon, Diane was already here. Diane had assured her that Marilyn would return for Mrs. Thomas's memorial if at all possible. The woman had been dear to Marilyn.

Since then, Diane had called the airline, and though she hadn't spoken to her friend, she was informed that Marilyn was hopping flights to get home as soon as she could. Possibly even by day's end. In addition, she'd swapped shifts so she could have the whole day off.

Mar also spent a huge chunk of the previous evening marking pages and letters with yellow sticky notes to identify what she wanted to copy tomorrow for Kevin. He had called last night to let her know the time of the meeting with the Gordons.

Now, it was time to rise and shine and get this show on the road. She dressed quickly and dashed into the kitchen where Mindy sat alone. "What? No Ken?" Mar opened the fridge.

"He'll be here shortly. So, no breakfast yet."

Mar rolled her eyes. "I do have food. I wasn't starving before you brought the chef home." She pulled out the jug of grapefruit juice. Only about an inch left.

"I know. It's just nice to have a thoughtful man waiting on me."

Mar unscrewed the lid and lifted it toward her mouth.

Mindy pointed. "You aren't going to drink out of that, are you?"

"Why dirty a glass when I'm going to finish it off?" Mar held it toward her friend. "Unless you want some."

Mindy waved her off. "I'll wait and see what Ken comes up with today."

Mar took a chug. "I'm off to get the copies made."

"Do you want me to go with you?"

"Nah. It's boring. Besides, when Ken gets here, if we're both gone, he might worry." Mar downed the rest of the juice. "Rose Swanson will be by later this morning. Another good reason for you to be here. If she arrives before I return, let her know I'll be right back."

Her friend saluted. "Aye, aye, captain."

"Also, Diane might call." Mar scooped up the pile of journals and letters she'd made the night before and headed out to her car.

Once on the road, she prayed this copying trip was faster than the last.

No lines, no mechanical issues, and no fussy customers. However, needing bits copied from here and there in the journals and letters, made the process tricky, but the employee was patient and efficient.

At her house once again, she spotted Mindy's Blazer sitting in front on the street, so Ken must be here. As she pulled into her driveway, a red van parked behind the Blazer.

That must be Rose. Mar's stomach twisted, anxious to converse with the woman.

A petite, smiling lady stepped out. When she made eye contact, her smile widened. Dashing up to Mar with open arms, she grabbed her in a bear hug. Well, as much of a bear hug as this small woman could muster.

"Oh, Margaret, I'm so glad you called. I've wanted to come for so long, but Paul insisted you had your own life. He said that since Beth was gone we shouldn't interfere, but ever since we moved back to this side of the mountains, I've had a hard time staying away." Rose stepped back and took a breath.

Mar wasn't sure what, or who, to expect, but she was relieved to recognize this woman and not just from the yearbooks. But from where? How was she connected to the family? "Just to be clear, you are Rose Swanson, aren't you?" Even as she asked it, she knew it was so.

Confusion played on the visitor's face. "Yes, dear." She touched her chest. "Don't you remember me?"

Mar felt silly. "Of course, I do." She just couldn't quite place her. It would come to her in a minute or two. "You've led me on a merry chase."

"I have? I never meant to. I'm sorry we lost touch." Rose tilted her head in a familiar way. "We saw you all as often as possible when you were young and some after your dad was killed, but as we get older life becomes more demanding. When we moved to the other side of the state, we saw less and less of you and your mom."

Suddenly, a light of recognition broke within Mar. "Auntie BJ! I never connected you as being Rose Swanson. I knew that name seemed wrong for you." How could she have not realized instantly who Rose was? "You used to come to visit my mom and that quiet man who sometimes came to see my dad must be Uncle Paul. I never put two and two together and got the right answer. I sometimes wondered about you. As you said, our lives change."

Rose threw her hands up. "Auntie BJ, that's me! I'm tickled you remembered what you called me when you were very small. Do you know why?"

"Something to do with my mom calling you BJ when you were little."

"Yes. My maiden name was Bjornson, and your mom thought it was funny to call me BJ. It spilled over into your generation. Do you remember sitting on the floor in your room, playing paper dolls? You couldn't have been more than five or six."

"I do. I always loved paper dolls."

"Me too."

Mar circled back to Auntie BJ's earlier comment. "There's nothing I would have liked better than having you interfere in my life, and I'll tell Uncle Paul myself when I see him."

Rose giggled approvingly. "He deserves it if you do, dear. He's much too cautious."

"Where is he? Didn't he come with you?"

"He had some things to tend to. He sends his regrets. We'll all get together after the New Year."

"Which is tomorrow." Mar hooked her elbow with her aunt's. "Let's go inside, and I'll introduce you to my friends. Then I'll ask you a million questions, so brace yourself."

Inside, she found Mindy and Ken in the kitchen, both at the stove, cooking. "Look whom I found outside."

Mindy turned with a smile then squinted slightly as though trying to place the woman. "You must be Rose Swanson. I know you, don't I?"

Mar chuckled. "A.K.A. Auntie BJ."

Mindy's eyes widened. "Oh my goodness. It's been so long."

"I remember you, Mindy. You two were—and looks like you still are—best friends. You lived a street or two over. Beth and I thought the pair of you were so much like we had been as children."

Mar motioned toward Ken. "Auntie BJ, this handsome gentleman is Ken Austin, Mindy's fiancé."

"Pleased to meet you, Ken."

"Likewise."

Auntie BJ glanced around with a smile. "I always loved this room best. Your grandmother was such a sweet lady and loved having your mom and me with her in here. She had hot chocolate and cookies when we came home from school in the winter or cookies and Kool-Aid in the summer. It was so hard for Beth when they were killed in that accident. It was doubly hard while George was in Vietnam. She missed them so much. Then you came along, and she was happy again. I wanted her to join us in Okanogan, but she wouldn't leave here. She was afraid to be away from the doctor, almost as if she feared her whole life would disappear."

Interesting about Dr. Thomas. She trusted him completely. And he had betrayed her.

Auntie BJ continued. "I still miss Beth so much. I can't remember a time she wasn't part of my life. I lived in the last house on this very block until Paul and I were married. I'm sorry, dear. I'm talking too much, and you have a million questions, so go ahead."

Mar gave her a hug. "Don't worry. You've already answered some of them by just remembering my mom and the grandmother I never knew. I've always loved this kitchen too, so I try to keep it a lot like it was all my life."

With an inquisitive expression, Mindy wiggled her eyebrows. "Have you told her yet?"

"I haven't had a chance to."

"Told me what?"

"Let's leave the chefs to their work and go in the living room."

Mindy bounced up onto her toes. "I'm coming too."

Ken held up the spatula in his hand. "Hey."

Mindy kissed him on the cheek. "You're a dream. Just call out if you need any assistance."

Mar settled on the couch next to Auntie BJ then reached into the Thomas envelope and carefully withdrew the photos. She handed them to her aunt.

Mindy sat on the edge of the chair on the other side of the coffee table.

Rose looked at one picture after the other. "You always were a beautiful baby and have turned into a beautiful young lady." She stopped at one image and referred back to the previous ones she'd perused. "There's something off here. I remember Beth telling me that you missed your third-grade spelling bee because you were sick. But there you are holding second place. You must not have been that sick."

Mar gave Mindy a knowing glance then flipped the photo over.

Auntie BJ scrunched her eyebrows together. "Who's Marilyn? That girl in the background?"

Mar tapped her twin, front and center in the photograph. "She's Marilyn."

Her aunt scrutinized the photo. "I don't understand. I was sure that was you. If she's not you, she could be your twin."

"Hold onto that thought a moment, and I'll come back to it. I'm hoping you have some additional pieces to this puzzle. I discovered a few things when I finally decided to sort out Mom's stuff. You were part of Mom's life when she was pregnant, so I called you for ideas of what actually happened and to help solve this mystery."

"Mystery? I don't know of any mystery involving your mom." Auntie BJ studied the photos for a moment then gave her head a shake as though to free the snapshots from her thoughts. "Ask away. I'll do my best."

"I found some of Mom's old diaries. One of the things she said in them was that she was pregnant with twins. What do you remember about what happened?"

"That was before Paul and I were married. In fact, your mom was worried about being the maid of honor. Thought she looked like a whale, waddling around. She was as beautiful as ever, but I wouldn't have cared as long as she was there for me. Anyway, she did have twins and managed to do it when I was away. One of them didn't live. She said the doctor took care of everything so she wouldn't have any lingering expenses. I don't know why she never said anything about it to you. Why is this such a mystery?"

Mar snatched up one of the pictures. "This is my twin. She didn't die. She's alive and well. She was raised by the doctor's niece and her husband." She laid out one photo after another on the coffee table. "And she's Marilyn, and so is she, and her."

Her aunt picked up the photos of both Mar and Marilyn. "I don't understand. These are of you."

"Only half of them. The other half is Marilyn, my identical twin sister."

Auntie BJ stared at Mar. Utter disbelief written on her face. "But that can't possibly be right. Your mother would have known if the baby had lived, and never—I mean *never*—would she have given her child up for adoption. You must be mistaken."

"It's the absolute truth. I'm going to talk to Marilyn's parents later today. At least, that's the plan."

"Are you certain this girl is your twin?" Auntie BJ squinted at one of the snapshots. "How did you find out who or where she was? Oh goodness. Now, *I* have a million questions myself."

"I'm positive she is. We're identical. Two different people have mistaken me for Marilyn. People who know her well, not just casual acquaintances. First, her next-door neighbor, then her best friend. She thought I was Marilyn playing a trick on her. It took a while to convince her I was Margaret Ross, not Marilyn Gordon."

Auntie BJ slumped back against the couch. "This is unbelievable."

While Mar conveyed the whole convoluted story, from finding the journals to Mrs. Thomas's confession envelope, Ken served them a hardy egg breakfast with the works.

"I'm beginning to believe you. Would you mind showing me some of the diaries so I can wrap my mind around this? Oh, dear." Her aunt sucked in a quick breath. "This is tragic. I feel so bad for Beth and

George. If she had come to Okanogan with us for your birth, you all wouldn't have lost the other baby. I should have insisted. I'm so sorry, Mar."

"It's not your fault. You couldn't have known anything like this would happen. What's done is done. I simply want to meet my sister and have her in the rest of my life."

Auntie BJ shook her head. "The Gordons really don't know Marilyn isn't their natural child?"

"I know it sounds impossible. It threw me for a loop too. I was almost ready to walk away and never try to contact Marilyn. Fortunately, my friends convinced me otherwise, and I believe Mom would want this, as well as Mrs. Thomas."

"Believing the other—Marilyn—had died at birth, what kept you digging? It seems like there wouldn't be anything for you to find."

"I guess I wanted to believe I still had some sort of family and needed proof before I could give up the dream. It was the lack of a death certificate for a Ross newborn that I couldn't shake. That's the one mistake they made because there was a death certificate for the Gordon child as well as the same-day birth certificate for Marilyn. The times are different, but the date is the same. Probably if he had switched the dead child, it would have satisfied us and been the end of the story, at least until the old lady died and told us everything."

Auntie BJ pressed her lips together. "That seems very careless of the doctor, and a mistake he wouldn't have likely made."

Mar nodded her agreement. "Near the Thomases' grave plot is a ground marker for a 'Baby G'. I thought it stood for 'baby girl'. I now believe it's for 'Baby Gordon'. Even in death, they wanted to hold on to their own."

"You certainly have had a rough time lately. I wish I hadn't let Paul convince me you were grown now and didn't need us poking our noses in your life." Auntie BJ hugged her. "Please keep me posted on how everything turns out. And when you are finally reunited with your sister, I want to meet her."

"Deal. And tell Uncle Paul, I want the both of you as a permanent part of my life." Having her aunt here was like having a part of her family back, even if she wasn't technically related. This woman was so much like her own mother had been. It felt good being together.

With lots of hugs and tearful smiles, Auntie BJ got into her red van and drove away, leaving Mar with the warm feeling of being loved and not alone anymore.

Hopefully, her meeting with the Gordons would go just as well.

Chapter Twenty

Mar waved to Auntie BJ until her van disappeared from sight. She wished she could spend the whole day with her, but too much would be taking place in the next several hours to dilly-dally on nostalgia.

Mindy came out onto the porch. "Aren't you cold out here?"

Not one bit. "I'm coming." Mar turned to go inside.

Mindy closed the door behind her. "A certain handsome doctor's on the phone."

That brought Mar back to the present, and she hurried to where Mindy had laid the phone on the end table. "Hello?"

"Hi. I hope I'm not interrupting."

"Not at all." A call from him was a welcome interruption.

"I know you have a lot going on today, but John Littlefoot is awake and wants to see both of us."

Excitement coursed through Mar. "That means he's all right and will recover."

"It's definitely a positive development. Do you have time?"

"Of course."

"We won't be able to visit with him very long. He needs his rest."

Her heart danced at the prospect. It was nice to have a distraction from her own recent drama. Nothing more would likely happen on the twin front until after Diane had lunch with the Gordons. Then later, she planned to pick up Marilyn and call with her reaction. "I just need to wait for Diane's call which should be any minute, then I'll head right to the hospital."

"See you then."

"I look forward to it."

"Me too." The hint of a smile seemed to color his words.

Mar sighed as she hung up the phone. She couldn't wait to see Kevin.

"You look forward to what?" Mindy stood beside her, wiggling her eyebrows up and down. "You have a hot date with an even hotter doctor."

Mar opened her mouth to refute the comment when the phone rang. She snatched up the receiver.

Mindy pointed at her and whispered, "Saved by the bell."

Mar put the phone to her ear.

"Hi. I just got to the Gordons' hotel." Diane's sunny voice came over the line. "I'm waiting for them to come down for lunch. I know you must be apprehensive. I am, too, a little, but this train has been set in motion, and it's rolling downhill, picking up speed. We can't stop anything now, even if we wanted to, so hang on for the thrill of your life. One more thing. Would you mind coming to the hotel to meet with the Gordons here instead of Dr. Drake's office?"

"Why?"

"I've been thinking about it, and I believe the hotel would be less threatening. If we meet at the hospital, Mr. Gordon might not go. He should be there too."

"Are you sure?"

"I am. Can you get the copies you made of your envelope back from Dr. Drake? That way we can show them the information the envelopes contain."

"Yes. I'll be seeing him soon to look in on a patient."

"Great! I'll meet you in the lobby at a quarter to three and get everything situated before I bring the Gordons down. Oh, here they come now. This will end soon, and the finish line will be worth the trouble."

"Oh, Diane, thanks for everything. I'll be at the hotel on time."

"I wouldn't miss this for the world. And in case you didn't already know, whichever way this goes, you're stuck with me as a friend for the rest of your life. Once a friend, always a friend. And thank you for trusting me enough to allow me to be a part of this."

"I couldn't imagine this without you. See you soon." As Mar hung up, she felt like laughing and crying at the same time. With a deep breath, she turned to face Mindy and Ken, filled them in, and hurried to the hospital.

Kevin met her at the entrance. "He's up on the fifth floor."

"I wonder why Johnny wants to see the both of us? Did the nurse give you any clue?"

He guided her to the elevator. "No. I guess we'll find out soon enough."

Getting off on the designated floor, they waved toward the nurse's station and entered the correct room.

Betsy sat in a plastic-covered chair by his side.

Though awake, Johnny looked banged up and groggy.

Betsy stood and gave Mar a hug and greeted the doctor. "I didn't expect to see you here again today, Dr. Drake. Is something wrong? I thought Johnny was doing fine." She returned to the chair and her vigil.

Kevin and Mar exchanged a questioning glance, then turned to the injured man in the bed. "We were summoned."

Johnny patted his wife's hand. "Bets, I had the nurse call Dr. Drake and asked them to come by while you're here. I have something to tell you, and I wanted them to hear it too."

"What is it?"

"I know Miss Ross has been a good friend." Though raspy, Johnny's voice seemed strong. "I've given you some really bad times, but you've always stuck by me, and you've been the best wife a fellow could ever want. Sweetheart, I want to tell you in front of them how I feel about you. I know booze didn't play a role in this accident, but I promise that never again will I take a drink. I want you to be able to trust me. I love you, Bets, now and forever."

The breath caught in Mar's throat. Her many months of prayers had been answered.

Kevin gave a firm nod. "We're all glad to hear that."

Betsy bent over and gave her husband a kiss on the side of his forehead that appeared to be uninjured. Tears rolled down her cheeks, but she was smiling. "Oh, Johnny, that's the most wonderful gift you've ever given me, except for our children, of course."

Johnny told of his plans. He felt that while AA and the alcohol rehabilitation programs were good, most of them didn't really address the special problems of Native Americans. "I'd like to go back to school and get training to develop a program for the northwest area to help our people fight against drug and alcohol abuse. I don't know if it will work, but I think it's something that's really needed. I would have probably responded better to a program that knew my ethnic personality instead of just that I was a drunk."

This news was as good as finding her twin.

Kevin nodded. "I think that's a marvelous idea. I'll do whatever I can to aid you in finding the training you need. *After* you have recovered. You need to get better first."

Johnny's eyelids drooped. "Knowing I have people on my side will help me get better."

Kevin tapped Mar's shoulder and inclined his head toward the door.

Mar squeezed Betsy's arm. "I'll check on the pair of you in a day or two." She slipped out of the room with Kevin.

Betsy had been able to see things in her husband worth sticking around for. It's too bad it took an accident like this to make the man decide to do more for himself, his family, and his ethnic culture.

The handsome Dr. Kevin Drake had some qualities worth sticking around for too.

Mar walked out into the corridor with him. "Oh, I almost forgot. We decided to meet with the Gordons at their hotel this afternoon. Can I get the copies of my envelope back? Diane wants to show it to them. And when Marilyn arrives later, I can give her the envelope addressed to her if you want."

Mischief danced in his green eyes. "Not a chance. Not only was I entrusted with her envelope, but this mystery has me intrigued. I want to see how it all plays out."

Mar drew more comfort from that than she would have expected. "All right. A quarter to three in the hotel lobby."

"I'll be there."

His declaration warmed her all over.

Chapter Twenty-One

A few hours later, Mar found herself alone in a small conference room off the second-level mezzanine that overlooked the hotel lobby. Her knees bounced like over-energized superballs. Mindy loitered outside but was nearby as a lookout to let Mar know when Diane and the Gordons arrived. Ken waited with Kevin in a sitting area. One option had been for Mar and Mindy to be there as well when the Gordons arrived, but the consensus was that might be too shocking. Best to ease them into things. Ken and Kevin were just the men for the job.

Mar nervously fussed with her hair. She stood and walked across the room.

The soft click of the door caused her to spin around. She let out a heavy breath. "Oh, Mindy, it's you."

"Who else?" Her friend approached and rubbed her back. "You're pretty nervous, aren't you?"

"Wouldn't you be?" Mar's whole life was about to change. For better or for worse.

"Diane and the Gordons just stepped off the elevator."

Mindy peered out through the crack in the door.

Mar held her breath.

"All's clear." Mindy opened it wider. "I'm right here with you."

"Thanks." Mar headed for the door.

Mindy pointed. "Don't forget your purse."

Mar snatched it and rushed out the door. "Thanks. If my head weren't attached, I would lose it today."

Mindy wrapped her arm around Mar's shoulders. "If you lose your head someplace, I'll get it for you."

Mar and Mindy stationed themselves around a corner, out of sight but near enough to hear what was being said.

Mindy whispered in Mar's ear. "It sounds like they've only dispensed with the introductions."

After Kevin had inquired about their flight and other pleasantries, he moved the conversation to the main point of the meeting. "I'm sure you want to know about your aunt. She didn't seem to suffer. She took a nap and simply didn't wake up. With help, I packed up her belongings, most notably a fur coat and photo albums. They are being held at the nursing home for you."

"Thank you," Ruth Gordon said. "I'll go by and see to them."

"I know a woman who would be happy to take whatever clothes and such you don't want to a woman's shelter."

"My aunt would like that. I'll let you know."

Kevin spoke again. "Mrs. Thomas may have had a premonition because she had the nurse call a young woman. A Miss Margaret Ross. Do you know her?"

Ruth's voice filtered around the corner but not as easily as Kevin's. "I've never heard of the woman. I don't understand. Why does that make you think my aunt could have had a premonition? I realize my aunt was quite advanced in years, so her death isn't too unexpected."

Mar peered around the corner to get a glimpse of them. Nothing more than the backs of two people's heads with gray hair.

"In her room, I found two large manila envelopes." Kevin spoke again. "One had your daughter's name on it and the other Miss Ross's. I've been entrusted with your daughter's. Seeing as how it is addressed to her, I can't turn it over to you nor open it."

"I can't think of what she would have left Marilyn."

Mar had to agree. No one would have imagined what those envelopes contained. She noted that Don Gordon remained silent, likely he was letting Ruth deal with her side of the family.

Mrs. Gordon continued. "She'll be arriving this evening. I'll let her know."

Diane spoke next. "I'll pick her up from the airport so you two can rest."

"Thank you, dear. That would be so helpful."

Mar's insides skittered about. She could meet her sister this evening. The thought both thrilled and scared her. Hopefully, Marilyn would be as eager to get to know Mar as she was her.

"As I told you upon your arrival, Mr. Austin is an attorney. He's here on behalf of Miss Ross."

Ruth again. "I'm confused. Is she expecting that my aunt left her something in her will?"

"I'll let Mr. Austin explain things."

Don leaned forward in his seat. "Why does this woman need an attorney?"

Oh, dear, he sounded defensive.

Ken spoke next. "Due to the nature of the contents of Miss Ross's envelope, we thought it prudent. I first want to say that I'm sorry for your loss."

"Thank you." Mrs. Gordon's words held a hint of uncertainty. But then whose wouldn't when faced with an attorney out of the blue?

Don Gordon settled back in his seat.

"As Dr. Drake said, Miss Ross received an envelope that appears to be identical to the one for your daughter. We assume the contents are identical as well. With Miss Ross's permission, I have been authorized to divulge those contents to the two of you."

Miss Ross? How bizarre to be repeatedly referred to in such a formal manner.

"There was information in the papers Mrs. Thomas left that will come as a terrible shock. One of the reasons we asked Miss Diane Oliphant to be here today is because she's a family friend and is apprised of the situation. Miss Ross became aware of certain facts even before your aunt passed away. I was planning a trip to Arizona to inform you of them."

"My aunt led a most uneventful life. Nothing about her could be worth all this fuss."

Not as uneventful as she thought.

Don Gordon spoke. "So, what's this supposed terrible shock?"

"Here is a copy of the contents of Miss Ross's envelope." Ken handed it to Ruth, but she passed it off to her husband. "There's no easy way to cushion the blow... but Marilyn's not your biological daughter."

Don jerked forward. "Not our daughter?"

"No, sir." Ken patted the air. "Mrs. Thomas details how the events occurred and her participation in them."

After a moment of silence, Ruth Gordon spoke. "Marilyn is my daughter. I gave birth to her. I remember."

"I'm sorry, but she's not. We have proof."

"What kind of proof?" Ruth shook her head. "DNA? Did Marilyn consent to that?"

"No. Not DNA, but undeniable documentation."

Don leaned back in his seat. "This all makes perfect sense." He didn't sound angry, almost relieved.

Ruth turned toward her husband. "What do you mean by that?"

"My blood type is O, yours is B, and Marilyn's is A. O plus B never equals A, therefore, I'm not her father."

Mar hadn't considered blood types. She too was A—*obviously*. She was dying to join the group. Should she before she was asked to?

"Why didn't you ever say anything?" Ruth's voice quivered.

"Because that would mean you had an affair, which I simply couldn't believe. I convinced myself that one or more of the labs made a mistake. I never blamed you. I was off to war. I was just so happy to have a child. Even if she wasn't mine."

"Oh, Don, she is ours. I know she is. These people are wrong."

Ken proceeded to explain the Thomases' actions on the day of the births.

"I don't believe you. This can't be true. As my husband said, there must be some sort of mistake."

Ken indicated the envelope in Don's lap. "Mr. Gordon, would you mind emptying the contents of that envelope?"

He did.

Ruth stared then recoiled. "What are those?"

Ken spoke. "We've made copies of pertinent information. The top one is a photograph of Miss Ross."

"No, that's Marilyn. Where did you get it? I haven't seen that one before."

"It's not. It's Margaret Ross. The items below it are the proof Mrs. Thomas left for the girls. In this envelope, I have the photocopies of the items Miss Ross uncovered two weeks ago, journal entries and correspondence which support the first evidence."

Don shuffled through the pages, appearing to scan them as he went.

Marilyn's mom burst into tears again. "How could I not know my child wasn't from my body? How could I not know that? I'm a terrible mom. How could my aunt and uncle have done this to me?"

Don hooked his arm around his wife's shoulders. "They did it because they loved you and knew you were having a hard time with so many miscarriages."

"Diane, Marilyn's your best friend." Ruth's voice held a panicked quality. "You've known her all your life. You can't possibly believe this isn't a picture of her."

Diane spoke. "I know it's hard to believe, but that is Margaret Ross. I've met her." She shifted her attention to Don. "Ruth will have an easier time with the flesh and blood proof. I think it's time to call Mar in."

Mar gasped and stepped out fully from the corner.

Chapter Twenty-Two

With her insides all tangled up, Mar approached. Diane clutched the older woman's hand.

Ruth's weary expression stretched into a wide smile. She lurched to her feet, pulling free of Diane. "Marilyn! I'm so glad you're here." She faltered for a second. "Tell them none of this is true."

Diane put her arm around Ruth. "This is my new friend Margaret Ross and Marilyn's identical twin. You can see for yourself the things we tried to explain."

Don gave a nod. "Pleased to meet you, Miss Ross."

"No! This is my daughter—*our* daughter. She's simply done something different with her hair. I gave birth to her. How could you imagine I'd ever think differently?" Shrugging off Diane's arm, Ruth opened her own, reaching out for Mar. "Tell them, dear, this isn't funny. Diane, stop this nonsense. It's gone beyond a game now. Why are you being cruel?"

Mar's heart ached for this poor woman. "This isn't a joke. I'm really not your daughter. I am Margaret Ross. Once I learned my mom had twins, I began looking for Marilyn. I realize this is quite shocking, and your head is probably spinning with questions."

Mr. Gordon smiled at Mar as he put his arm around his wife. "She's not Marilyn."

"But . . . but . . ." Mrs. Gordon looked frantically from Mar to Diane. "How? There can't be two of you. Marilyn was only one baby, and I had her. I've had her all her life. You can't be twins."

Don helped Ruth back into her chair. "It's true. Your aunt and uncle must have thought they were doing us a favor."

Ruth's hands shook. "But she's ours, Don. She's ours."

"Mrs. Gordon, are you going to be all right?" Kevin stood and closed the gap between himself and Ruth then took her wrist, checking her pulse. "Take a few deep breaths for me."

Her breathing slowed. "Dr. Drake, are you sure this isn't some mistake? You're a physician, this just isn't possible."

"She looks pale." Diane put her hand on the woman's shoulder.

"Nothing seems obviously wrong." Kevin sat on the chair next to Ruth. "Mar, will you get Mrs. Gordon some water, please? There are pitchers on the other side of the mezzanine."

Mindy raised her hand. "I'll do that." She hightailed it away.

Diane took Ruth's hand. "I know this is unexpected, but even if Mar had tried to keep it from you, everything would have come to light soon anyway when Marilyn received the envelope your aunt left."

Ruth pressed her fingertips to her forehead. "None of this makes sense."

Mindy returned with two glasses of water, handing one to the shaken woman and the other to her husband. "You'll feel better once you've taken a sip or two."

Ruth complied.

Mar thought it best if she remained quiet for the time being. Mrs. Gordon was having a hard-enough time without her forcing the matter. Mr. Gordon, on the other hand, had readily accepted it. He had known something was amiss, apparently, for some time.

Ruth turned a pleading gaze on Kevin. "Dr. Drake, tell them what they're saying is impossible."

"I'm afraid it is possible, Mrs. Gordon. I know you've always believed Marilyn was your natural daughter, but the truth is, she's not. Miss Ross has not only documentary proof that your child is her twin separated at birth, but your aunt has confirmed it and actually confessed how it was done."

Mrs. Gordon took a long drink of water. "Diane, help me? They don't seem to understand what I'm telling them. Marilyn is my own baby."

Diane patted her arm. "Though unbelievable, it's true."

Ruth turned to her husband. "I don't know anything about any other child. How can you, of all people, believe these strangers?"

"I know it's hard, darling, but your aunt confirms it." Don turned his attention to Mar. "What do you want from us?"

Mar cleared her throat. "Nothing. I merely want to be part of my sister's life . . . if she'll let me. This is a lot to take in. Why don't you go up to your room and read through everything?"

With a distraught expression, Ruth Gordon stretched an arm toward Mar. "Marilyn, I'm your mother." Her voice cracked, and her pleading gaze seemed to probe Mar's soul. Could it be possible she thought her daughter had suffered amnesia, and she herself could bring her back to sanity?

Mar went to the woman and knelt before her. "I'm sorry. I'm not your daughter. When she arrives, you'll see for yourself."

Ruth's features turned from anguished to perturbed, and she gripped Mar's hand. "I've had enough, Marilyn. This is *not* amusing." She wrenched Mar's hand over and studied her palm. She gasped, then grabbed her other hand and studied it. "Where is your scar? The one you got when you fell off your bicycle."

Tears pooled in Mar's eyes at this woman's distress.

"You're not . . ." Ruth pulled her shaking hands away and turned her attention to Diane. "Where's Marilyn? Where's my daughter?"

Diane's expression held compassion. "She's on a flight and will be here this evening."

Ruth took a sip of water. "If Marilyn's not . . . not . . ." She brought the glass to her lips but didn't appear to drink. "If everything you say is true, then what happened to *my* baby? I had a baby. I know I did."

Mar spoke as kindly as possible. "You did. A little girl. She didn't survive, but I believe she's buried near Dr. Thomas in a grave marked 'Baby G.'"

A tear rolled down each of Ruth Gordon's cheeks. "I had such a terrible time having a baby. I lost several." She cupped her hand on the side of Mar's face in a loving way only a mother could. "Marilyn was a blessed gift. We love her very much."

"I know you do."

"You must hate us."

"No. None of this was your doing. Marilyn is fortunate to have you for parents."

"Mom! Dad!"

As Mar stood, she turned and faced herself.

Chapter Twenty-Three

Time seemed to slow. Silence reached Mar's ears. No one else existed. Only herself and her twin. As though suspended between heartbeats.

Marilyn's smile faded, and she narrowed her eyes. "What's going on here?"

Mar sucked in a huge breath she hadn't realized she'd been denying herself.

"Oh, Marilyn, you're here." Ruth rushed to her daughter. "We weren't expecting you until this evening."

Marilyn kept a wary gaze on Mar. "I hopped an earlier flight. A perk of being a flight attendant. Who is this?"

Don smiled at his daughter. "We have quite a story to tell you."

Diane came up beside Marilyn. "Mare, this is Mar, your identical twin!"

Marilyn's expression turned to a grimace. She faced her parents. "You had twins and gave one away?"

Mar stepped forward. "No! None of this was their fault. They didn't know anything about it."

Don motioned toward a chair. "Have a seat, sweetheart, and we'll explain."

"I'll stand, thank you."

Mindy held Mar with her gaze. "I think Mar should show her the photos."

Ken pointed to the information Mar had copied from her mom's stuff. "We should start with the documentation. The facts."

Kevin patted the envelope in his lap. "The material from Mrs. Thomas is the linchpin in all this."

"May I explain it to her?" Ruth's voice had a slight quiver. "She's my daughter." She looked up at her husband. "*Our* daughter."

Don hooked an arm around his wife. "Do you think that's such a good idea? Perhaps I should."

Marilyn shifted her attention from person to person as each pleaded their case.

Mar could feel the confusion swirling within her twin. Everyone pulling Marilyn in a different direction, and her trying to decide whom to side with but lacking all the information to do so. "Stop." The chattering continued, so Mar tried again but louder. "Stop!"

Everyone turned to her as their words trailed off.

"I know how overwhelming this all is, and I was able to mull it over alone." Mar picked up the information she'd copied from her mom and put it back in the large envelope. She handed it to Marilyn. "This is what I discovered from ou—my mom." She snatched the Thomas envelope from Kevin without asking and handed that to her sister as well. "Take this and go read through everything. I know how incredibly hard this all is. It's a lot to take in. When you are ready . . ." She dug a pen from her purse and scribbled her phone number on one of the envelopes. ". . . give me a call." Slipping her purse under her arm, she turned to her friends. "Come on. Let's leave this family to sort this out in private."

"Wait." Marilyn held her gaze. She remained silent for a minute as did everyone else.

Mar held her breath. What was Marilyn feeling? She probably wanted all the answers immediately, as Mar had.

Hugging the envelopes with one arm, Marilyn motioned toward Mar. "Would you come with me?"

As Mar moved to follow, everyone else shifted as though they planned to come also.

Marilyn waved her hand at them. "Only her." She marched around the corner Mar had originally concealed herself behind. She stopped and turned but didn't say anything.

Mar waited until her sister was ready to speak. That was so weird to have a real sister. She wanted to throw her arms around her but restrained herself out of compassion, knowing what it felt like to be thrust into this situation.

Finally, Marilyn found her voice . . . sort of. "I . . . I . . . I don't even know where to start. You look exactly like me. This is surreal."

"I know, but also fantastic."

"You said none of this was my parents' fault." Marilyn furrowed her eyebrows. "How could they give you away?"

"They didn't. Dr. and Mrs. Thomas are the ones who separated us at birth without the knowledge of either of our mothers. The short version is your mother had trouble carrying a healthy baby to term. Her baby didn't survive. When my mom had twins near the same time, the Thomases swapped you for their child."

Marilyn glanced toward the corner. "They aren't my real parents?"

Mar's heart ached for her twin. "They are every bit your parents. They raised you and love you."

Marilyn shook her head. "Did your parents agree to this?"

"My dad was in Vietnam as was yours. My mom was alone and worn out from delivering two babies. The Thomases told her the second baby didn't survive. That made it easy for the Thomases to present you to your parents. They never knew you weren't their biological child. Mrs. Thomas explains it better in her envelope."

Marilyn squinted at Mar for a long time. "So, we really are twins. I have a sister." A huge smile broke across Marilyn's face. She dropped the envelopes and wrapped her arms around Mar.

Mar hugged her back, so grateful her sister was accepting of her. Tears flowed down her cheeks.

Epilogue

June 1999

As Mindy and Ken drove out of sight, Mar heaved a heavy sigh. The majority of her maid-of-honor duties were complete. Mindy's wedding dress and other belongings were safely tucked inside her car. She took off one shoe, then the other. Though rough, the blacktop parking lot felt surprisingly good on her aching feet.

Marilyn came up beside her and wrapped her arm around her shoulder. "You done good, sis." She shook her head. "I'm still not used to that."

Mar wasn't accustomed to it either but perhaps a bit more than her twin. "But it's something worth getting used to."

"Definitely." Marilyn had switched her schedule to domestic flights based out of Sea-Tac. She had moved in with Mar so the pair could get to know each other better.

Mar felt as though she was living with herself, even though they were raised apart with no knowledge of each other. They were frighteningly similar, a lot of the same likes and dislikes. "I never imaged having a sister-twin would be this amazing."

"Me either."

"It's like there was a piece of me missing that I didn't even know was absent."

"I know what you mean." After a pause, Marilyn continued. "I have a demand and a question."

"Okay. What if I don't want to give in to your demand or answer your question?"

"Not an option in either case." Marilyn held out her hand palm up and wiggled her fingers. "Now, time to cough it up."

"Cough what up?"

"The ring. I know he gave it to you. I've seen you sneaking glimpses of it all day." Marilyn shook her head. "And don't try to deny it. Being your only blood kin, he asked my permission. He's so old-fashioned."

Mar grinned and bit her bottom lip. "We didn't want to take any focus away from the happy couple." Tucking her shoes under her arm, she lifted the hem of her dress and removed the pouch attached to her calf. In it, she had her car key, lip gloss, and her ring. She removed it and slipped it on the appropriate finger.

Marilyn held Mar's fingers and tilted her hand back and forth. "Is that a black pearl?"

Mar nodded. "He researched and found that Margaret means pearl. I've always loved pearls." The diamonds surrounding the pearl twinkled in the sunlight that had broken through the clouds.

"You two make a perfect couple."

"I agree. So, what's your question?"

Marilyn gazed off across the parking lot. "Who is that fox talking with your handsome doctor?"

Mar chuckled. "His cousin, Keenan."

"Is he single?"

"Yep. Let's go get the two of you introduced." Mar hooked her arm with Marilyn's and strode across the parking lot with her twin.

Six months ago, Mar was alone in the world. Now, she had the best sister ever and was engaged to an awesome guy who made her heart dance.

All the puzzle pieces of her life interlocked together . . . perfectly.

Mary Linn Chase was born in Bremerton, WA, on Sept. 5, 1933. In 1943, she and her family moved to Silverdale, WA. She graduated from Central Kitsap High School in 1952. During her school years, she was active in the music department, playing the clarinet and saxophone in band and concert orchestra. She married Air Force sergeant Don Russell, had six children, and traveled to Idaho, California, Japan, & the Azores, but she always returned to the Puget Sound area. After 15 years, she divorced Russell and married Frank Lum, inheriting two children. They also had one and adopted one of their granddaughters for medical reasons. She loved writing, dining out, her family, and music. Upon finishing this novel, she tapped her head and said to her sister, Sarah, "The one I have in here is even better." She went blind, so she wasn't able to write that story. She passed away in 2013.

Bestselling, award-winning author **Mary Davis** has over forty titles under her belt in both historical and contemporary themes and all featuring a little to a lot of romance. She's had characters running around in her head as long as she can remember but never considered being an author until adulthood. Her first two novels were published in 2000, and she has been going steady ever since. She's been married for thirty-nine years, has three adult children, three adorable grandchildren, and a senior foster cat. When she's not writing, you can find her doing one kind of craft or another.

Find her online at:
Books2Read: https://books2read.com/marydavisbooks
GoodReads: https://www.goodreads.com/author/show/8126829.Mary_Davis
BookBub: https://www.bookbub.com/authors/mary-davis
Newsletter: https://marydavisbooks.ck.page/

BOOKS BY MARY DAVIS

The Quilting Circle Series
The Widow's Plight
The Daughter's Predicament
The Damsel's Intent
The Débutante's Secret
The Lady's Mission

Other Books
Mrs. Witherspoon Goes To War
Newlywed Games
Titanic: Voyage of Intent

Find these and other Mary Davis books at https://books2read.com/marydavisbooks[1], then click on the cover.

---

1. https://books2read.com/marydavisbooks,then

Milton Keynes UK
Ingram Content Group UK Ltd.
UKHW040819141124
451205UK00001B/69